Locked Door
Shuttered
Windows

WHITE
TREE
PUBLISHING

Locked Door Shuttered Windows

J Stafford Wright

Original writing ©1985 J Stafford Wright
This publication ©2013 C Stafford Wright

ISBN: 9-781-4791-1543-3

PUBLISHED BY
WHITE TREE PUBLISHING
28 FALLODON WAY
BRISTOL BS9 4HX
UNITED KINGDOM

INTRODUCTION

This book was written shortly before the author's death in 1985. J Stafford Wright was a respected theologian and author, and former Principal of Tyndale Hall Theological College, Bristol.

Well known for many books on the Bible and Christian doctrine, this is Stafford Wright's only full work of fiction. It was initially believed that he had left an incomplete manuscript of this book, but a complete work has now come to light. In it the author, my father, had got as far as making the occasional handwritten correction to the first third of the book, sometimes adding a few words for the sake of extra clarity. My son Jonathan and I have done minimal editing on the remaining two thirds of the book, of which I know my father would have approved, being careful to leave the whole story intact.

This supernatural story by a prominent Christian minister and writer will challenge those readers who see the work of the devil to be solely one of destruction. The plot is ingenious, and the ending memorable.

Details of other books by J Stafford Wright, currently in print from White Tree Publishing, are shown on the back pages.

Chris Wright
Bristol
England

CHAPTER 1

Although I didn't know it at the time, my story began like Job's in the Bible. "Now there was a day when the sons of God came to present themselves before the Lord, and Satan also came among them. The Lord said to Satan, 'Whence have you come?' Satan answered the Lord, 'From going to and fro on the earth, and from walking up and down on it.'"

In the account that I am writing in this book, a later conversation between God and Satan took a very different turn. The Lord spoke. "You have done more than going to and fro on the earth. You have been attacking my people for thousands of years."

"And you have attacked mine. That is why I have come to talk to you, if I dare. I remember how, when I first opposed you, you threw me and my supporters out of heaven."

"You wanted the throne of the universe for yourself. But you may speak freely, and I will listen."

Satan looked round on the angels who had gathered, and then spoke. "Why need we continue to fight? I have come to suggest a diplomatic settlement. If you are willing."

He paused to see the effect of his words.

"What have you in mind, Satan?"

"You will remember that I proposed a settlement two thousand years ago when you came to earth as man. I am addressing you as the Three in One. When I tempted you in the wilderness, I made a very generous proposal. I told you that if you would admit my claims to the so-called fallen world, I would hand it over to you. You wanted the world, and it could have been yours."

"I died on the cross for it."

"But I offered you a shorter and less painful way. Your Bible describes me as the god of this world. I have many followers, and we could have reached an agreement for a joint rule. You might have bargained for even more, but you didn't. Yes, you died on the cross, but what good has it done you? You know what the world is still like. Is it not time we started working together, and had a proper control?"

"My answer now is as it was then: Be gone, Satan!"

Satan stepped back. He remembered that, when he finished tempting Jesus in the desert, "Be gone" meant that he had to go, and it had been set down in black and white in the records as "then the devil left him."

But this time Satan stood his ground, although he sounded hesitant. "Let me dare to speak once more. I have much experience of the world, although I admit your experience has been greater than mine. But there are things in your government of the world that puzzle me. I wouldn't wish to criticise, but ..."

"But what?" God said sternly.

"… but I feel that *together* we might achieve what neither of us can do singly."

"You mean that you could govern the world better than I can."

"I have only used the term Together."

"But even so, you are thinking you could do better — if you ruled it on your own."

Satan nodded. "Yes, I believe I could run the world in a good way — if I had complete freedom."

"How can you prove that?"

"If I could have a community of men, women and children who are people of goodwill, without being tied to you as Christians, I believe I could do with them more than you have been able to do. I don't ask for them to be sinless, since that is impossible. But I would rule them in my own way, and I believe I would succeed."

"Succeed in what way?"

"I would make them happy and obedient, and turn them into a viable community."

"So you would teach me a lesson, Satan? Suppose I allow you. Where would you set up your community?"

"I have travelled through the universe, and there is a planet some millions of light years distant from earth. Its climate is not so different. It has plants and creatures not so very different either."

"I know it," said God. "I created it and the life on it, but without humans. You can guess why."

For once Satan was taken aback, before he slowly understood.

"Yes," God said, "I foresaw that you would request this

experiment. All right, you may have a free hand, if you can transport your community there."

"Then I am free to rule it as I wish?"

"Yes, quite free."

"When you let me tempt Job to make him lose his trust in you, you set a limit each time on what I was allowed to do. Is there a limit here?"

"Yes," answered God, "there is just one. If any of your people turn to me and pray, then I shall be free to help them."

Satan bowed very slightly. "I agree", he said. "However, I can promise that none of them will turn to you. I shall choose my company with care."

God said, "The audience is over. You can go."

CHAPTER 2

Poor old Job was never told of the scene in heaven which led to his troubles, and it was some time afterwards that I was told of what I have just related. But in what follows, I will be describing my own experiences.

My name is John Longstone, a bachelor of thirty-two when this story begins. When I left school, I won a university scholarship and read classics for my first year. During this year, I had an experience which I believed to be a conversion to the Christian faith. So with a view to possibly being ordained, I switched from classics to theology for my second and third years.

Theology at university at that time was beginning to argue about Christian beliefs, and I didn't feel more Christian at the end of the course, perhaps even more confused. However, I went on to a theological college, and in due course was ordained in the Church of England. Overall, I think I was a fair preacher, and was able to help people who needed the help that a parson can give.

One day to my surprise the principal of my former

college gave me an invitation to return as a member of staff to teach theology. I was glad to accept, because although I had preached the old-fashioned Christian beliefs in my curacy, I had pushed aside the problems of some modern thinkers. I thought that to be forced as a lecturer to study these doctrines more closely would clear my mind considerably.

I had tried to be satisfied with orthodoxy. Now the various new approaches frightened me. For two years I lectured along the lines of "What the Bible teaches", but being forced to read all the latest serious works I gradually found myself unable to teach. I tried to stand orthodoxy on its head by saying one thing and meaning another. I knew what I doubted, but what did I believe? Was the Resurrection true? Was the Virgin Birth a fact? Was Jesus Christ truly God? Did his death on the cross mean anything?

Then one morning I woke up with what seemed to be nothing less than a second conversion. I suddenly saw the liberating truth — there *is* no God. If there is no God, all these other problems are nothing. No God, no God-Man, no atonement, no resurrection, and of course no prayer and no sacraments. I was free at last. I thought of the verse in the Gospels, and laughed: "The truth shall make you free."

I saw the college principal after breakfast and told him I had lost my faith, and must leave. I didn't tell the students why I was leaving, as somehow I felt that this was my own conclusion about the Christian gospel, and they must find it for themselves, if ever they did. I saw the bishop and resigned my Orders. He did his best to talk me back into the Christian faith, but I assured him that I already knew all the standard arguments.

I was fortunate enough to have inherited quite an amount from my parents, so I didn't immediately need to find fresh work. I was able to follow up something that had interested me for many years. I suppose I must have a streak in me that some might call "spiritual", although I prefer something like "non-material". That is to say, from a child I've sensed that there is something beyond the material world and the way the brain sees it.

I had looked in poetry and art, but now I turned with enthusiasm to the study of parapsychology and the psychic realm. It became a substitute for religion with me, a religion without obligations, without superhuman demands. There was no God, but there was an exciting inner world to be explored, much of which might explain some of the phenomena of religion, and dispose of the unique claims of Christianity. I mean, Christian and other experiences might well be purely natural, and have nothing to do with a god.

I was absorbed in the field of extra-sensory perception, clairvoyance, clairaudience, telepathy, ghosts and poltergeists, when something strange happened.

CHAPTER 3

As far as I remember, it was a Sunday evening. Yes, I had been subconsciously aware of distant church bells as I settled in my deep armchair with a new book on some interesting psychic cases.

I'd been wondering for a day or two whether psychic energies could account for all the phenomena in which I was interested, or whether one would need to postulate the actual existence of spirits, whether spirits of the departed or of an order of demonic, or even beneficent spirits. Could such spirits become involved with people and events in this world? I mean to say, were poltergeists unleashed psychic energies of someone in the family, or the pranks of a noisy spirit, which is what the German word poltergeist means?

I was half asleep, and the book fell on to my lap and wakened me. The atmosphere had suddenly turned cold. I instinctively looked up. I was in my favourite chair on one side of the fireplace, while a smaller armchair for visitors was on the other side.

In this smaller chair sat a tall man in black. I could tell he was tall by the length of his legs which he had stretched out in front of him. When I had sat down, the chair had definitely been empty, my front and back doors were bolted, and my sitting room door was shut. How had he come there?

In my present state of mind I could think of only two explanations: a hallucination or a ghost. Mind you, the two could be the same thing. I was surprised by my own calmness.

The man dressed in black seemed to guess my thoughts. "I'm hardly unsubstantial enough to be a ghost, and if you shake hands with me you'll find I'm not a hallucination."

He leaned forward and put out his hand. Hardly realising what I was doing, I put out my own and gripped his. His hand was cold as ice.

"Who are you, then?" I demanded.

"Someone who knows you very well. I've been watching you for quite a time."

I stared at him. "But I don't know you. In fact, if you'll excuse me, I've never set eyes on you before. And it beats me how you got in here in the first place."

"We have our ways," he said, with a smile.

"Well, what do you want with me?"

"A good question. I'd better begin at the beginning. I've observed that you no longer believe in God, although you included theology in your degree, and have preached and taught as a Christian."

It was a puzzling opening, and I couldn't see where it was leading. But I answered him. "That's quite true. I discovered there were only psychological and traditional reasons for supposing there's a God. Perhaps you know something about psychology?"

"I know as much as you do, and more. And parapsychology too. You're interested in that?"

I nodded in bewilderment.

"Tell me then," he said, "do you believe in the spirit world?"

"I really don't know," I said, forgetting the strangeness of his arrival, and warming to my subject. "Curiously enough, it's something that's been in my mind for several days. Surely everything can be accounted for by the projection of psychic force from the inner mind, without postulating the existence of spirits."

He smiled. "Suppose I told you that I am a spirit — materialised of course. Would you believe me?"

"If that's a hypothetical question, I would have to weigh it up before I answered. But if you want me to believe that you are a materialised spirit sitting in my armchair, I would have to say No."

He continued to smile at me. "I *am* a spirit."

I now felt frightened, not because he might be a spirit, but because he might be mad, and possibly dangerous.

Again, he must have guessed my thoughts. "Don't worry, I'm not out of my mind."

"Then who are you? For goodness sake, tell me."

"Then will you listen with an open mind to what I'm going to tell you?"

I nodded agreement.

"When I said I'm a spirit, I meant it. But I am more than a spirit: I am the most powerful of all spirits."

"I used to believe that God is the most powerful spirit, but that's out for me now, as you know."

"Of course. My name is not God. I am Satan."

You know the shivers you get when it sounds as though there are footsteps on the stairs in a dark old house? I couldn't speak, until gradually the thought came back to me that I was dealing with a schizophrenic with delusions of super personality. I began to wonder what excuse I could make to get to the phone in the hall.

His smile now seemed to me to be the mindless smile of the insane. He spoke. "You said you would listen with an open mind."

I took the risk of a little psychological tact. "You don't want to be Satan. Satan is hopelessly bad, and you want to be good."

He sighed. "I see I must give you a lesson that as a lecturer in theology you ought to have known. People blame me for being the source of evil. In fact, the stuff men and women think of as evil — murder, theft, rape, and other things of a similar kind — actually come from within people themselves. Even Jesus knew that, when he talked about what came from the heart. It's true I may put someone in the way of those sort of things, but my work is to direct the plans of individuals and the world into what I know could be good for them."

"In what way?" I asked, strangely now half-believing him.

"Do you remember how I tempted Jesus in the wilderness? Jesus was evidently thinking out there what his policy would be, but he wouldn't listen to my suggestions. He was certainly a miracle worker, but he was stupid enough to starve himself almost to death by refusing to do a simple miracle for himself, and turn stones into bread. I told him the world would be impressed if he were to throw himself off the temple roof, and let the angels, whom he professed to believe in, carry him gently down to the courts below. Even I would like to have seen that. In the end, to show how honest I am in wanting what is good for the world, I offered him a partnership with myself."

"That's rather a new thought, isn't it?" I said. "That's not how we imagine you."

"Then you haven't understood me at all. I know I can run the world in a proper way, and make it a happy place to live in. But only if I have an absolutely free hand. Good people go on insisting that their alleged God must somehow be brought in, while bad people — I use the current terminology — let themselves go in such a way as to spoil the plan for the rest."

"That's all very well, but you *have* been pretty ruthless in attacking those who regard themselves as the people of God."

He held up his hands as though horrified by my suggestion. "Only if I've been driven to it by attempts to attack me and my rule. When I lose my followers to the other side, I am naturally angry with the people who take them away."

Once more I was puzzled. "You make it sound as though you and the so-called God have very much the same aims. You both want to make the world run well."

"You could put it like that. But the difference is this. Those who believe in a God say that God must be at the heart and basis of everything, if the world is to be put right. My aim is to build a good world without depending on any idea of God at all. He's not needed."

I turned over in my mind this new concept of Satan as the reformer, as well as the enemy of God. It began to make sense. Whether it was his talk or some force of his personality, I found myself accepting the fact that this person sitting opposite me was Satan himself. I didn't shudder at the idea. I could believe in him without believing in God. I had already decided that there might be invisible spirits. But I still wanted to know what he wanted from me. He answered my unspoken question.

"I am about to demonstrate an experiment. I won't say *try* an experiment, because I know I shall succeed. I need someone to help me, and I believe you are the right man."

"Why me? I'd better tell you straight away that it's one thing to throw God over, but it's another thing to go in with the devil. I don't like it."

"Then I'm sorry. I want a man of maturity, who has seen from the inside all the ideas about God and discarded them, a man who has studied psi. I want a man who is prepared to remake mankind *without* God, by helping someone who has had many thousand years of experience. I want you to join me as the go-between between myself and humans who are less instructed than yourself. I give you my word, I won't ask you to do anything against your conscience. You can keep that. But think it over carefully. I'll be back this time tomorrow for your answer."

Suddenly the armchair was empty, and I was left with a feeling of utter exhaustion. If this unexpected visitor had indeed been Satan, he had evidently drawn on my psychic energies in order to materialise.

CHAPTER 4

I need not say it was the hardest decision I had ever needed to make. From one point of view it was completely ridiculous to think of going in with Satan. I thought of Faust who sold his soul to the devil. But stories like that belonged to the days when people believed they had immortal souls that would suffer in hell for all eternity. I no longer believed in an immortal soul, and certainly not in hell. If death is the end, one must live to the full here and now. So if Satan could offer me the good life, why not take it?

Satan — if indeed it had been Satan — had given me a new picture of himself as an absolute but beneficial ruler. I thought over what I remembered of the New Testament picture of him from the days when I taught in college. The Bible of course is biased, but it speaks of Satan as "the god of this world" and "the prince of this world", which is more or less what he had told me. So he must be concerned with the proper government of the world. It wouldn't be in his interests for everyone and everything to become as bad as possible.

He's called the deceiver, but that's because he opposes the alleged God, since he naturally tries to refute this God's claims. He's called the tempter, and he had already explained this. His aim is to inject decisions into the mind, as he tried to do with Jesus. I saw the Bible picture of Satan in a new light. It seemed to me that he had already done a pretty good work in the world, but obviously he was looking for something new.

By this time, I was more or less convinced that I would go along with him, although I determined to keep my mind open until I knew more about his plan.

Promptly at six-thirty, he was there in the armchair.

"Yes," he said, anticipating my unspoken thoughts, "you naturally want to know the plan. I warn you, it will sound crazy, but I assure you it can be done."

"I'm listening," I said.

"Your scientists tell you that life is probable in other parts of the universe."

"Yes, but only probable. They haven't found any."

"There isn't much to find. I know of only one small distant planet in this galaxy that has life, and that's not human life either — only creatures somewhat similar to those you have here. But its climate and atmosphere are near enough to what earth has, so humans *could* live there."

"So what?" I don't usually use such vulgarisms, but it seemed the only thing to say — a mixture of disbelief and curiosity.

"I'm planning to plant a colony of humans there under my direct rule. I want you as my agent — if you will join me."

Can Satan suffer from paranoia? I wondered. With some sarcasm I rejoined, "Not a very long journey, then?"

He answered me in my own coin. "Quite short. Just a few million light years."

"Is that all! What time does the train start?"

He didn't answer, but stared hard at my face, giving a sense of pressure which I struggled to resist.

He spoke again. "If I can transport you all there, will you come?"

"Yes," I cried, "yes, I'll come. But the thing's impossible."

"I told you that one of the reasons I chose you was that you knew something about psi."

"That's true, I do. But what has that got to do with it?"

"You've read about teleportation."

"Yes, I know it has happened, but nobody knows how solid objects can pass through solid walls into a room, and how occasionally people have suddenly appeared many miles away from where they were last seen."

"I can make it happen. If a solid body can be dissolved and rebuilt, it is no harder for it to pass to a spot millions of light years away than into another room or another place on earth."

I gasped. "So you really are serious." I felt my bluff was being called, and I now regretted my hasty agreement to go along with this unbelievable plan.

"I am serious. Deadly serious. And I want you to come with me."

My reading had inclined me to accept impossibilities.

Suddenly the whole thing made sense. "I'll come."

"Thank you. Then I can put you in the picture. We need about eighty people, singles and families. We must have a mixed community of ordinary people, intellectually and socially. It would be good if we could have a complete set of total goody-goodies, and keep them good, but there aren't any such people. We have to start with faulty material — with apologies to yourself — and mould them into a happy community. We certainly can't have any Christians. You will do most of the interviewing, and you must make certain that no one attends church, or sends the children to Sunday school or takes any private interest in Christian books. Even one adherent of the Christian superstition could wreck the whole plan. We shall demonstrate that utopia can be achieved without God. Are there any questions?"

"Yes. How are we going to find the right people?"

"We'll try an advertisement in the local evening paper. You'll have to interview anyone who seems promising material. Try this: *Individual and family volunteers wanted for constructive community experiment. Congenial surroundings. No Christians need apply.* That's roughly what we want to say. We'll put a box number, and letters will be forwarded to you for preliminary vetting. Then you and I will make a selection for interview. I suggest we hire a hotel room for that purpose."

"How can I describe you in the interviews? I can hardly advertise you as Satan."

"Call me the Anonymous Scientist. You can say I'm anonymous because of the jealousy of my scientific colleagues."

17

"If you can get us all up to that planet, what will you supply there?"

"I've told you there are mammals, birds and fish that are much the same as you have here. I've arranged for houses to be built out of local stone and wood."

"Who on earth will build them?"

"No one on earth. I have many workers."

This was the first time Satan had hinted at other spirits beside himself. "We must be realistic," I objected. "What about heat and light?"

"You can use electricity. There is a waterfall that will drive turbines to generate all you need, but you must choose men who can maintain it."

"Won't we need to buy things? Food and suchlike?"

"We can manage that. We can issue tokens for money, and get things teleported from earth for a shop. You might look out for a shopkeeper in the applications."

"One other question. Has this planet got a name?"

"Not yet. Can you make a suggestion?"

"Well, as it's up in the sky, could we call it something like Heaven's Home?"

Satan put his hands over his ears. "Never let me hear you mention that name again!"

"I'm sorry. I wasn't thinking. Our planets have used up most of the Greek and Latin gods and goddesses. But what about a classical king — say Priam?"

"Sounds good. Priam it shall be. You can get on with the advertisement, and I'll be looking in."

Once more the armchair was empty, and once more I felt drained out. And rather cold.

CHAPTER 5

When the advertisement appeared, replies soon came in. It was interesting to read them, but not easy to pick out the possibles, far less the probables. However, I was confident that we would be better able to sort them out in the interviews.

Curiously enough, in spite of the words in the advertisement, several Christians applied. They were surprised at such discrimination in this day and age, and argued in their application letters that Christians were needed for the stability of a community. I need hardly say they were not invited for interview.

I rejected those, and also some other applications because the applicants gave so few particulars of themselves. Others wrote at considerable length, and I sensed that some of these were rather too weird to be reliable members of the community.

Fortunately, there was a reasonable choice of professions. We needed a doctor, and there was a good GP and his wife. I rejected a solicitor, since, if the experiment worked, disputes would be settled by a committee. We were looking out for a shopkeeper, and found a husband and wife who kept a general store. There was an application from a printer, and another from a general handyman, another from a farmer. I thought these would be useful.

Two teachers — a man and a woman — who enclosed good references could cover the basic needs of children, if books could be teleported. I was particularly glad to find a shoe repairer, whose daughter was a librarian. Two for the price of one, as it were, and I guessed we should have a library. There were plenty of what one might call average individuals and families with various jobs and interests. I decided to keep to families with no more than two children, plus several grannies and grandfathers to keep a balance.

Satan constantly scrutinised the list, and made suggestions. When the time came for interviews, he left them to me, but told me that he would be present, though invisible.

Only one journalist got hold of the advertisement. He worked for the paper in which it appeared, and came to interview me about the plan. I simply told him that I was only an agent acting on behalf of a gentleman who wished to remain anonymous. It was my task to pass on the names of people to him. Fortunately, this interview was evidently too dull to print.

Naturally, the first question anyone asked was about the "constructive community experiment" referred to in the advertisement. Of course, I didn't frighten them by talking of outer space, but kept to the experiment, devised by a scientist, for satisfactory community living in a village in pleasant surroundings. Stress would be on simplicity of life, without being overloaded with any modern gadgets, or being caught up in the rat race of city life. Most of them fell for this, although two or three backed out when they found there would be no cars.

When we had made our final decision, we had to fix the date and time and method of the teleportation. I discouraged anyone from selling up, in case they decided to return, although Satan was confident that the project would be such a success that no one would want to come back to earth.

Looking back, I am sure Satan used some hypnotic influence on their minds to keep them from worrying about their houses, so that they didn't even contemplate renting them out while they were away. They were unconcerned when I told them on June the twelfth that June the twenty-fourth, the Summer Solstice, would be the date of departure. Even when I told them not to pack anything, since everything would be supplied in the new community, no one objected.

Although a few seemed a bit restless at being kept so much in the dark, most accepted the wishes of an anonymous eccentric scientist to keep everything secret until the last minute. Actually, they had to wait until almost the last minute before they received final directions by letter. These instructions sounded so strange that again only some sort of hypnotic influence from Satan could have induced anyone to follow them.

The letter said they were about to take part in a rather strange experiment. To this end, at midday on June the twenty-fourth they must relax as completely as possible.

Quiet music would help. Then without any concentration they would start to repeat aloud softly, again and again the single word *Priam*. They must not attempt to leave the house, and they would be taken very soon to the new community.

Meanwhile, Satan instructed me to go to a stone circle some miles from my home. He explained that while the repetition of the word *Priam* would produce some psychic power, we might need further psychic force. So at the stone circle I would be at the centre of an old focus of force, which by concentration I could mobilise. I had already understood from my reading that people of old sensed lines of force and places where the forces built up, and made use of these in various ways. Now it was my turn to use them, because much psychic energy would be needed for this transportation.

At midday I stood in the circle and did my best to tune in to the vibrations around me of which I gradually became more and more aware. It was a beautiful day, with the sun overhead in a blue sky flecked with clouds. Time became irrelevant. I was in the past and the present simultaneously. One moment I was standing on the green grass in the centre of the circle. I had no sense of motion, but the next moment I was standing on the grass in the centre of a village green, staring at houses in the street.

The effect was the same as when the scene changes in a film. I had not moved, but the film had changed. I was seeing a fresh picture in which I was taking part. It was still a beautiful day, with the sun overhead in a blue sky flecked with clouds.

As I stood staring, people came pouring out of the houses. I could hear them shouting "What's happened? Where are we?"

Some of them recognised me, and rushed on to the green. They pressed round me, all the time looking in a bewildered way at the strange surroundings and at one another, since this was the first time they had met together. I was their only point of contact. I had to reassure them.

I forget now just what I said, for I was almost as staggered as they were. But I told them we had had an experience that had never been given to another person on earth. Through the skill of my master, the Anonymous Scientist, we had somehow been transported through outer space to a planet called Priam, many billions of miles from earth, but like earth in many ways. The interiors of the houses were as near as possible identical to the houses they had left on earth.

Meanwhile I told them I was still the agent of the great scientist who would be able to supply us with what we needed. Together we must build a new and happier life. I think I sounded terribly formal, but I was exhausted by the psychic forces that had invaded me at the stone circle.

The people parted as I moved across the green. On the other side of the street I could see a house that looked very like the one I had left behind on earth. Indeed, it had a brass plate on the gatepost, with the word Agent. I went up the path. The front door was unlocked. Inside it was almost exactly the same as mine at home.

A large and a small armchair each side of the fireplace reminded me of my first meeting with the gentleman in black. My own books were in their own bookcase. I looked out of the window and could see people still moving about uncertainly. Two or three were talking together. Others were obviously making their way back to what was now to be home.

The thought came to me that we were like children arriving on the first day of their first term at school. We were strangers to each other in a strange environment. We had to form new friendships and build a new life together. Priam was now our Alma Mater. *Floreat Priam!*

CHAPTER 6

At a later date I saw Dr Peter Faber's notes that he started writing on the day after we arrived on Priam. I reproduce them here, to show the reactions of one member of the party who, unlike myself, was very much in the dark about all that was happening. This is what he wrote:

I find it difficult to understand how I have come to be mixed up in this strange affair. I can trace the steps, but why on earth did I keep agreeing? The one word that keeps coming into my mind is "pressure". I'm not easily influenced as a rule, but this was a strange sort of inner pressure, almost as though I were being hypnotised into saying Yes.

Perhaps I should blame it on depression. For some time I have been getting more and more depressed over the state of the world, and over the laws and restrictions that governed my medical practice. I could see that my wife was worried about me, and the antidepressants I give to patients had no effect on me.

One day I had a visit from a patient who came to me fairly

regularly, a Mr Richard Halliday. He came in with more excitement than usual.

"Well, doctor, this may be my last appointment with you. I'm pulling out of the rat race."

"I wish I could," I said. "Where are you going?"

"I've more or less promised not to say, but there's no harm in showing you this advertisement."

He pulled a crumpled piece of paper out of his pocket, and smoothed it down on my desk. This is what I read:

Individual and family volunteers wanted for constructive community experiment. Congenial surroundings. No Christians need apply.

There was a box office number.

"Do you mean to say you've applied?"

"Yes, and been accepted. If you'd like to try, I don't think it'll be too late. Nothing has been finally fixed about the date for going."

The whole advertisement struck me as the work of a crank, but I began to feel pressure on my mind.

"Well," I said, "I'll get the particulars and ask my wife. Presumably we'd go together."

At lunch I broached the subject. My wife's face changed for a moment, and she put her hand to her heart.

"What is it?" I said in alarm, jumping up. "Are you all right?"

"Yes, of course. It was just that something came over me when you spoke. It must have been excitement. Yes, yes, of course we must apply. We both need a change, and the children are grown up."

We talked it over, and in the afternoon I wrote a letter. A reply came in less than a week, and my wife and I were asked to go for an interview with a Mr John Longstone at a large local hotel. We were both impressed with him, but I can't say why, since on looking back he was extraordinarily evasive in his answers to my questions. Yet, curiously enough, he left us with the impression that we would be joining a scheme which would take us right out of the rat race to a simple, satisfying life in ideal surroundings.

Mr Longstone gave very little concrete information, although he assured us that he was the agent of a brilliant scientist who had everything worked out. Now I'm wondering just who this mastermind is. We have never seen him, nor do we know his name. This fellow Longstone seems to be managing everything.

Somehow, we fell in with his seemingly bizarre plan. All the time the sense of inner compulsion was driving us on to do what surely we would have resisted with calmer thought. We were told not to discuss the project with anyone, but simply to say that we were going on holiday, and to make any necessary arrangement accordingly. So I arranged for my son to take on my practice, as he did sometimes.

Then we wondered whether, after all, the whole thing was a hoax, especially when we were given instructions to prepare ourselves on June 24th by withdrawing on our own in quiet meditation, and reciting the two syllable word "Priam" again and again. But once more, the inner pressure drove us to agree.

We were told not to pack anything to take with us. That seemed strange, but the thought came to me that this would be a way out for the super-scientist if the scheme failed. We would simply be left to carry on as though nothing had happened. Yet it sounded absurd. Could we assume that everything we needed would be provided — if we ever arrived at our unknown destination? I couldn't help feeling all the time that we were behaving like silly children playing some imaginary game.

At the appointed hour we sat down opposite one another in two armchairs, and began the mumbo jumbo. What happened next is beyond me. One moment we were there, and next moment we were sitting in the same room in the same chairs, and yet what *seemed* to be the same was somehow different.

We got up simultaneously and moved quickly to the front door. All seemed the identical until we stepped out into the street. Then, in place of the houses opposite, we found ourselves staring across a sloping village green. Other doors were opening, and people ran out, calling, "What's happening? Where are we?"

Someone shouted, "There he is!" and I saw Longstone standing on the green, looking as bewildered as we were. People rushed towards him, and we followed. But all we got from him was reassurance that all was well, and somehow we were now on a planet called Priam in outer space. It didn't make sense, yet we were certainly in a strange place, and it might as well be called Priam as anywhere else.

Longstone said we would find everything we needed in our houses, and when we had all settled down he would be available to answer questions and solve problems. I have never seen a crowd quieted so quickly. I'm not surprised, if they all felt the same inner pressure as was moving my wife and me to keep quiet and trust Longstone.

When we returned to our house, there was my name on a plate at the gate, announcing my medical qualifications. Inside, the house appeared to be virtually a replica of the one we had left. What puzzles me is what has happened to us all.

The mad scientist — which is what I am inclined to call him — has evidently solved the problem of UFOs, if indeed they exist. He is not limited even to the speed of light. We travelled at the speed of thought, as though mind had taken over matter. Or is the whole thing a case of mass hypnosis? That's a thought that disturbs me some nights when I am unable to sleep.

I wrote these impressions of mine yesterday evening. The sun, so similar to our one on earth, set soon after eight o'clock. We stayed up talking until ten o'clock and then went to bed. Yes, by electric light. We are already beginning to accept life here as normal. Indeed, we went to sleep in our new/old beds, and slept soundly.

I woke before my wife, as I usually do when we are on holiday. I generally creep out early and spend a quiet half hour in the country. I opened the front door and looked out. Everything was still, and there was no one about. The sun had just risen. I walked up the street, with houses on my right, and the green on my left, then past other houses further on.

When I was clear of the village I came to a little wood, and made my way in among the trees. Not far off I heard the sound of running water and walked towards it. I came across a stream running from left to right, and followed it until suddenly I was on the edge of a lake. A line of sun sparkled across it, and away from the bright streak a fish jumped in the water.

At home I sometimes relax when I find a scene of this kind. I'm not a religious man, and I don't believe in a god, but I believe in the healing power of nature. And after the uncertainties of the past few weeks, I thought I would sit here and soak myself in the sheer beauty of the scene.

But something was wrong. Instead of the peace that I was looking for, my soul (what a stupid word!) was troubled by a feeling to which I cannot put a name. It was as though nature herself was somehow crooked, and could no longer give me peace. I felt restless, and had to stand on my feet again. Sitting was impossible. I walked along the lakeside, but the whole thing had turned nasty — that seems the only word to use. I even had a sense of fear, and kept looking over my shoulder. The words from Coleridge's *Ancient Mariner* came ringing into my head, and I repeated them aloud.

> "Like one that on a lonesome road
> Doth walk in fear and dread,
> And, having once turned round walks on,
> And turns no more his head;
> Because he knows, a frightful fiend
> Doth close beside him tread."

Of course, I don't believe in fiends, frightful or otherwise. Nonetheless, I turned round and quickly made my way back the way I had come.

There were now a few people up early and out in the street. One stopped me and asked if I knew where he could buy a newspaper. To his dismay I told him I had no idea. When I reached my house my wife was up, cooking eggs and bacon on the stove as she did at home. When we went over the house last night, we had found the larder well stocked with familiar foods, though where they had come from in outer space I had no idea. Perhaps a good breakfast would drive away my fears. Like the man I'd met in the street, I missed my paper.

After breakfast I set out again, this time turning to the left. I had not gone far before I came across the village shop. The window appeared to be well stocked with useful things, and I went in. The shop itself had a number of shelves along two sides. The counter was opposite the door, and in the space behind there were other shelves, loaded with tins and packets. Sides of bacon hung from hooks in the ceiling, and I could see packs of meat and vegetables in a long container: refrigerated, I supposed.

An elderly man and woman (husband and wife, as I guessed correctly) stood behind the counter, serving three customers. I felt in my pocket for money and pulled out, not the familiar coins, but alloy tokens stamped with 1, 2, 5, 10, 50 and 500. How they had got there I cannot tell. They just have to take their place with the other mysteries.

The shopkeepers seemed bewildered when I spoke to them when the others went out, and we were alone. They were as mystified as any of us. They had been in their own shop, I forget where, and they had been transported with the rest of us yesterday. Longstone had prepared them for carrying on their work in new surroundings, and indeed this shop was not unlike their own. I asked about money, and they told me that there was some sort of a bank next door. At the moment everyone apparently arrived here with tokens in their pockets, but Longstone had told the shopkeepers that more tokens would be supplied at the bank.

I was at a loss what to buy, but asked for cigarettes. They apologised, and said that the agent had told them that the purpose of the new community was good health for everyone, and that his boss had said that smoking was bad and addictive, and he had no time for anything that would weaken the community. So they had no cigarettes. I bought a tin of soup.

Before going home, I looked in at the so-called bank. There was only one sad-looking cashier at the counter, and he told me there was no one to help him. He had been a cashier in a big bank in England, but had thought that this would be an opportunity to change. But he hadn't pictured a bank that merely issued tokens. He brightened a little when I suggested that some customers would want to open accounts.

He had been transported to a small apartment above the bank, and had found on the table details of the token system. The strong-room was piled high with tokens. He was appalled to read that to open an account a person simply had to ask for a number of tokens, the ration being 600 points a month. He had to issue and stamp a card for each customer, and keep a duplicate in the bank. He remarked that this wasn't what he called banking at all. He sounded even more depressed when I asked for my first 600.

I left him to his gloom.

I went home and persuaded my wife to go and draw her own 600 tokens, for I have no confidence in the future of our community. Nor, incidentally, has my patient, Richard Halliday, who brought me into this strange affair. I saw him leaning over his gate as I went back to what I must learn to call "my home".

I called "Good morning."

"Not all that good," he answered. "I wish I'd never come. The sooner I'm back, the better I'll be pleased."

But will we ever be back?

CHAPTER 7

I need not add to Dr Faber's memoirs. They cover much of what I would have needed to explain. For myself, I was inundated with callers on that first day, all asking much the same questions.

I wished that Satan had been there to give the answers, but he had told me he intended to be out of sight as much as possible, but that I could always communicate with him by what one calls a hot line — except that there was no actual line, only a sort telepathy if I spoke to him out loud.

Of course one of the first questions the people asked was, "When can we see the boss?"

I explained that he was a shy man who had always believed in working from behind the scenes. How true that was! In addition, he still had many concerns that needed his presence on earth, although he would doubtless teleport himself here whenever it was necessary. Meanwhile, he had given me authority to make decisions.

The next most frequent question was, "How long are we staying here?"

My answer was to remind them that they had volunteered to come of their own free will, and they couldn't possibly start thinking of return yet. In my own mind, I wondered whether return was even an option.

Some asked whether it was safe to leave the village and go out into the country. I was able to assure them that there were animals about, but none that would attack humans, not even small children. Again, Satan had told me that Christians on earth didn't seem to see through the fallacy that their god, who called himself a god of love, allowed mankind to be attacked and killed by wild beasts. Satan had assured me that he had put a controlling force upon all dangerous creatures, not forgetting snakes.

"You see," he said, "I want my people to think of me as one who is wholly concerned for their welfare."

Some seemed anxious about lack of the media, for there were no newspapers, or radio and television sets. I pointed out that one of the aims of our community was simplicity and self-containment. To know what was going on upon earth, thousands of light years away, would be disturbing and upsetting, even if it satisfied our curiosity.

I added that I hoped to arrange a local press, which would write up our own doings. I was not sure yet whether the printer we had recruited would agree to work a simple printing press — if one could be teleported.

There was one question which proved to be important later. This was, "What about crime?"

I could only say that we had tried to choose members who would be law-abiding. If a baddie had slipped through the net, he would be dealt with severely if he was guilty of any crime.

"Who would try him?"

I tried to look confident. "This would depend on what the community decided. I would like to get everyone together to elect a council. And the council will draw up rules, including rules for the treatment of offenders."

When I was alone again, Satan appeared. He had evidently been listening. "Good answers!" he said. "I like your idea about a council. Put up a notice asking anyone interested to come to a meeting tomorrow evening to decide about the running of the community, including the election of a council. It doesn't give them much notice, but at present they aren't likely to have fixed up other engagements. By the way, you had better get elected yourself. It ought not to be difficult, as they all know you, even if they don't know one another."

He disappeared.

We had been provided with a school building, with three classrooms and a large hall. Obviously the hall was the best place for the meeting I hastily arranged. I counted thirty-five people present, and concluded that some of the rest were baby-sitting at home. I was elected chairman by acclamation, after Dr Peter Faber proposed my name. So I sat down on a beautifully carved chair on the platform, with an equally fine table in front of me. Satan was evidently not one to put up with anything shoddy. I could see a pad of paper and a ballpoint pen on the table.

I rose to make a short opening speech before asking for questions. "Ladies and gentlemen, companions on this great adventure, I thank you for your support in voting me to the chair." (Hear, hear!) "I want, in the name of our leader, to welcome you. You have all had a chance to look around, and like myself you must be amazed at the miracle that has brought us here, and the amazing supplies of all that we need. One might say it is a second Garden of Eden."

At this point I felt my hand picking up the pen and writing at lightning speed on the pad. I would have felt self-conscious if it had not been that the attention of the audience was drawn to a thin-faced man at the back of the hall, who rose to his feet and called out, "You don't believe all that Bible stuff about Adam and Eve, do you?"

I joined in the general laughter, meanwhile glancing down to see what I had written. Although I had certainly written it, the writing was in a strange hand: *Don't say that name again.*

I took the warning, but it gave me an idea. Perhaps my hot line to my boss could take the form of automatic writing as well as telepathy.

I went on, "It may be that there will still be things you wish to have up here. If so, you have only to let me know. Ask, and you shall receive."

I was rather pleased with that. It was, I know, a quotation from the Christian Bible, but it brought an unexpected comeback from a sad looking lady in the second row.

"Do you mean we can have whatever we ask for?"

"A good question. One must use one's common sense about asking. There may well be things that aren't good for us to have. For instance, I mustn't ask to be a millionaire."

"Why not?" called a voice.

"Another good question. If I ask for a million tokens, it wouldn't be good for my character to find a million dumped on this table. On the other hand, I might be answered by being shown how to work hard enough, and skilfully enough, to become a millionaire in twenty year's time. No, what I mean is that any *reasonable* request will be answered as fully as possible."

I paused for a further question. As no one spoke, I amplified my previous answer.

"There is a difference between being spoon-fed and being ready to work for what we need. This isn't a holiday camp, with everything handed to us on a plate. Most of you can do at least one thing, and can teach others how to do it. Some of you know a trade. Then teach it to others. If you have children, help the family who are now farming on the hill to milk their cows and gather in their crops. If you want a newspaper, see if you can help gather the news, and give a hand with the printing press that has arrived unexpectedly this afternoon. It's a simple model that will be slow to use, but Joe Penny seems happy to work it, even though it's old fashioned. We must try to be as self sufficient as possible."

"What about a trade union?" someone asked.

"Why not. You can decide that for yourselves. But, if I may suggest, a single inclusive union would be better than a lot of little ones with only one or two members in each."

"I haven't seen a pub," said someone.

"With so few of us here we won't need one. We can buy drink at the shop."

Then came a curious question. "Do we all have to be good?"

I tried to remember what I had read in the past about ethics. "What do you mean by 'being good'?"

"Well, just being good. You know what I mean."

"I'm not going to give you a lecture on morality, but so far as I can see it's like this. You can please yourself so long as what you do doesn't interfere with other people. You are responsible to yourself alone. But if you start spoiling someone else's life, you'll have to pull in your horns. Our scientist, who drew up the plan for our life, has no intention of letting his plan be wrecked. He has brought us here to live a satisfying life, and I think he'll want to see it worked out."

My hand wrote, and I looked at the message. It said *Good*, and soon afterwards I closed the meeting. I had promised to accept suggestions for a small executive council when we had come to know each other better.

CHAPTER 8

I met Dr Faber next morning after breakfast as we were both out doing some more exploring.

"Do you mind if I join you?" he asked. "It doesn't look as though anyone's needing my attentions. My wife will be joining me when she's washed the dishes and tidied the house. It amazes me how we've got electricity already. What with a cooker, vacuum cleaner and even a washing machine, it's a home from home. By the way, you're not married are you? I've not seen a wife around."

"No, I'm a self-sufficient bachelor. I've cooked my breakfast and done the housework. I'm out for a walk to find out more about the place."

He joined me, and we strolled for a minute or two in silence.

"You managed the meeting last night, but there's still a mystery in my mind about the man behind all this. Excuse my asking, but is there a boss at all? I mean, are you the man who's worked all this out? How, I don't pretend to know."

I laughed. "That's a compliment, but I'm not that clever. Yes, there is a boss and I'm nothing more than the one he's chosen to be his agent."

"Does that mean you understand how he's worked all this?"

"Only vaguely. I know he's mastered the power of using mind over matter. I know quite a bit about psychic force, but only as a hit and miss affair. He has evidently mastered it completely, and has somehow transported us all here, and created this village and everything in it."

"Created? That sounds like the old idea of God."

"He certainly hasn't created them out of nothing. He's had to use existing material and adapt it."

"Pardon me if I seem inquisitive, but I suppose it's because as a doctor I like to find out all I can about my patients. You seem to believe in psychic experiences. Are you in fact after all a religious man?"

As I hesitated, he went on. "I noticed last night your allusion to the Garden of Eden, and then your quotation of "Ask and you shall receive," the words of Jesus, if I remember rightly."

I laughed. "It's understandable you should say that. I was in fact an ordained clergyman and a teacher in a theological college, and this was one of the things that turned me from the Christian religion and shattered the faith I once had in God. I felt a promise like that should work out every time. My mother had a serious illness, and then my father. I asked for their recovery, but it just didn't happen. I found it impossible to go on believing in God at all. God was only a concept that could neither answer prayer nor satisfy an inquiring mind."

The doctor nodded. "Roughly the same thing happened to me. I couldn't get over the facts of suffering and death, whether my patients prayed or not."

"Exactly. And I couldn't find that any theologian could give me an answer that satisfied me."

The doctor went on, "So you think your boss can deliver the goods in a way that Jesus couldn't. I noticed you had to hedge a bit last night."

"Of course I couldn't promise that everyone will get immediately whatever they asked for."

He looked thoughtful, and added, "I wonder whether Jesus thought the same. But that sounds rude to your boss. I'd be interested to know more about your job before you threw it up."

"I told you I was a teacher of theology, even though I believed less and less what I was teaching. In fact, I think I may have given my students more doubts and hesitancies than faith."

"I like honesty," said the doctor.

"Well, it was a bit of a tension, and I was glad to leave the whole thing. I told you my mother and father died. I've no brothers and sisters, so I inherited everything, and my father was a very rich man. I don't want you to think that I just sat in an armchair all day. I've always had an active mind, so I was able to work at my hobbies, and especially to give time to psychical research and the study of the inner world, not to mention a bit of dabbling in magic and spiritualism."

"But not religion?" queried the doctor.

"No, not religion. I found I could explain most of the ideas of religion by psychology and psychism."

The doctor smiled. "And I found everything could be accounted for by the brain and the body."

Perhaps I shouldn't have said it, but I did. "So you didn't think you had to postulate the devil as the source of all the illness you had to deal with?"

"Don't try to pull my leg. Who believes in the devil nowadays?" He swung round and looked behind him. "Who was that laughing?" he said.

"I didn't hear anything," I announced truthfully, thinking he was joking.

"Ah well. Getting imaginative after all we've been through. But it's funny. I really thought there was someone behind us."

I don't remember what we talked about after that. I sensed some restraint between us. Presently he turned and remarked that his wife would be expecting him. He didn't seem to want me to walk back with him, and I went on alone.

I wanted to see the electricity turbines that I guessed must be somewhere up in the hills. As there were no cars in the community, there was no need of a road once leaving the village street, but the doctor and I had been walking along a track which had been made through the grass. Incidentally, the grass on this planet apparently never grew to more than an inch or two in height.

I came to a place where the track divided. I left the right-hand path to be explored later, and took the left-hand up a hill. I don't know what I was expecting, but when I came over the brow of the hill I found myself looking down into a steep valley with a swiftly flowing river at the bottom.

Away to the left I could see and hear a high waterfall thundering into a narrow gorge. Here a solid stone building housed what were evidently the turbines for generating electricity. Not enough, of course, for a city, but enough for our small community. To me the generation of electricity was a mystery, but I knew we had a couple of electrical engineers in our number, and I made a mental note to send them up to see how much maintenance would be needed.

It was a fine picture. I always enjoy the sight of running water. Where the river went to, I couldn't say. Dr Faber had mentioned a stream and a lake, but this river was obviously bigger than a stream, and I found later that it swung away from the village by a horseshoe curve.

I retraced my steps, and made up my mind to go a short way down the other fork in the track. It soon became a typical country lane, with high banks on each side covered with strange flowers. Then it ran straight into a wood, dark and sombre, with branches of trees meeting overhead, so that I was in a dark corridor. The shapes of the branches reminded me of Arthur Rackham's strange pictures that I could remember from a childhood book. It was weird enough to be frightening, and I had no heart to go further.

"Another day," I said to myself, and turned back to find the sunshine again.

There were no birds in the wood, but outside they were singing in the bushes and trees by the way, and a hawk soared overhead.

CHAPTER 9

As once I had studied theology, so now I found myself trying to grasp Satanology. I've made up the title, because this was not just Demonology. I had not yet had any direct encounter with other spirits than Satan himself, although Satan had told me that his workers had constructed what we needed for our life on Priam, such as our houses and even the electricity generators. I had gathered that none of these had been created out of nothing, but had either been made out of materials already on Priam, or had been teleported from earth.

What concerned me was to understand the ways of Satan himself. I had come to realise something of his plans before we left earth, but now that I was seeing him in action I began to appreciate his ideals for our community, and could compare these with what I had once been led to believe were God's plans for the world.

There was a certain similarity. Satan planned a stable society, which meant that he had to control divisive elements, including many of those things that I used to call sins. He would allow a certain amount of personal pleasures, but not things that would disrupt the family or damage personal health. These would spoil the plan that he had for a good world without God. Thus, he wouldn't supply cigarettes, and if anyone had asked for recreational drugs I've no doubt that he would have said No. At the same time I found myself wondering how he would deal with any unpleasant family troubles that might arise.

I could see that it was important that Satan should appear in a good light if he was to achieve his object. I remembered that the Bible somewhere described him as posing as an angel of light. Surely if the people knew that the Anonymous Scientist, their boss, was actually Satan, the whole community would have gone to pieces, with a licence to sin as they pleased.

Meanwhile the nearest they came to Satan was through me, and I flattered myself that in me they would see only the highest standards. In fact, some of them, like the doctor, half suspected that I myself was the Anonymous Scientist who had engineered the whole project, and I was aware that I was treated with a certain awe. I have to admit that I found it slightly gratifying.

Where Satan's methods differed from what I had been taught about God, was in his readiness to answer prayer. He encouraged people to ask for what they wanted, and nine times out of ten he gave it to them at once. The plan was that anyone could come to me with requests for what he or she wanted. I noted these down on a list, and at a certain time each day I sat down alone in my house, and opened up my "hot line" to Satan.

He was obviously listening as I read through the list aloud, and by next morning the things that had been asked for appeared in the shop, where they could then be bought, or sometimes they appeared directly in the home. As I've said, unlike God, Satan granted these petitionary prayers nine times out of ten, and gave exactly what was asked for. It was interesting to me to discover the reasons for any refusals.

One day the doctor's friend Richard Halliday asked for a revolver and ammunition. He told me that he wasn't too happy over one or two members of the community. He needed the gun for protection if he were to be attacked, and it would be useful for policing if trouble broke out.

Satan's prompting to me said, "Strike that out!"

Next day Halliday's neighbour appeared at my door in an excitable state. "I hear Halliday's getting a gun. We can't have just one man with a gun in the village. I'll have one too."

I assured him that Halliday had not been given a gun, and he wouldn't be getting one either.

At this point I began to wonder. Here was Satan acting as the God of the Bible would act. He was working for peace. Well, why shouldn't Satan and the Bible have at least some similar ideals? In the mythical kingdom of God there would be complete peace, since people killing and threatening one another would destroy the kingdom, just as they would destroy Satan's community here. That made sense.

There was sense in some other refusals too. Nearly everyone at some time or another asked for a newspaper so as to know what was happening back at home. These prayers were always refused. I wouldn't have minded a paper myself, but I could see that news of life on earth would be unsettling. I found myself remembering a sermon I'd preached from the Bible text, "If they had been mindful of that country from whence they came out, they might have had opportunity to have returned. But now they desire a better country, that is an heavenly."

I could see that there would almost certainly be no opportunity to return, but Priam was a good place in the heavens. In fact, the Bible text promised a *future* pie in the sky, whereas Satan was giving us the pie here and now.

Occasionally people asked for the impossible, such as television. Since there were no transmitters, there would be no point in watching a blank screen. I suppose we might have had video recordings, but again there would have been unsettling reminders of life on earth, including the disturbing acceptance of violence and sex. Well, I had told everyone that they would be leaving modern technology behind if they decided to come.

After a time I found an unexpected result of Satan's bounty creeping in. The mood of, "You only have to ask for it, and you'll get it" did no good to a number of those who came with their petitions. I even detected a certain rivalry, so that when one person had something, a neighbour would demand, and receive, something better.

I never discovered the principle on which personal possessions were brought to us. Some, like Dr Faber, received directly what they needed. Other requests were delivered to the shop, and had to be paid for at a fixed price.

It was becoming clear that there was already a difference between what I will call the rich and the poor. Some were saving their tokens so that they were able to buy things that were more expensive, others spent their tokens as soon as they got them.

I couldn't help thinking that if Christians on earth had found their God answering prayers in this way so quickly, there would have been many more converts.

Gradually our village organised itself. Small groups came together for mutual help, and individuals emerged as leaders and organisers. The children went to school, and the two teachers appeared to be efficient. We had several good amateur gardeners.

General health was good, meaning that my doctor friend had an easy time, and he and his wife explored the country around, and reported to me places that I might feel were worth seeing. Satan had chosen an excellent planet for our purposes. It had a variety of scenery, flowers, birds and other animals, and a mixed climate of sun and rain with a temperature that varied little.

So time went on.

CHAPTER 10

I have already said that some of the people regarded me as the real boss, and when I went out I was conscious that I was bathing in the reflected glory of Satan. This made me wonder whether I might indeed rise even higher. After all, Satan had chosen me for a great responsibility, but he had many secrets that were hidden from me. If only I knew them, who knows what I might become? Could I even challenge Satan himself? I hardly dared to consider the possibility.

Were there more secrets that I might discover somehow? The word *secrets* reminded me of an attractive old house on the edge of the village. It had the name *Secretum* on the gatepost. The heavy wooden door was locked, and the windows were shuttered. I knew the door was locked because I had seen several people try it.

I had not investigated it myself, because there was a large board outside, saying *Strictly Private* and *Out of Bounds*, and I thought I would be setting a bad example if I were seen going up the garden path.

Now I began to wonder what secrets the locked and shuttered house contained. Was this a house that would make me wise with a wisdom that would enable me to compete with Satan on equal terms? At this point I noticed something that I had not seen before. Beside the fireplace in my sitting room hung a key. It was a very fine large key, with a handle beautifully wrought, hanging from a ring at the top. For the first time I realised that it could be the key for the locked door of Secretum.

Why had it been given to me — at least, not given, but put in my charge? After all, I was the leader, and the warning notice might not apply to me at all. It might be necessary for me to know what was inside. Indeed, it could be a duty that I owed to the community.

I walked over and examined the key closely. I now saw the word SECRETUM engraved in tiny letters on the ring. I had assumed the metal to be iron, and I suppose it may have been, but when I touched it, it had a curious warmth about it which I could not account for. I pulled myself together. What was I doing? I had never dared to disobey Satan's orders before.

I continued to look at it.

It is true I had not disobeyed Satan's orders before, but how did I know that the notice outside the house really meant Satan's orders for *me*? After all, the house was different in style from others in the village. Then I thought it must be meant for us to look at and admire. The builders, whoever they were, had probably built that house as a replica of an old country house, complete with crumbling rendering, to make Priam feel as though it had a friendly past. But it might not have been built to be inhabited, only as a sort of ornament, and it might be dangerous to go into it.

In the end I returned to my original idea. There must be some secret in the house, and there was no reason why I should not know it — especially as I already knew so much from my studies and from Satan himself. I would at least have another look at the house. At this moment I thought the key rattled on its nail — no doubt, as I assured myself, due to a draught. I took it down and went outside.

There was no one in sight as I walked casually up the street to the house. I paused and gazed at it. In spite of its obvious age, it would be a good house to live in, and maybe Satan would allow me to move into it. With a plant climbing the old wall beside the door, it was strangely beautiful to look at, in spite of the shutters at every window. Deep down I knew it contained a secret that would make me wise. Indeed, I could be as Satan, knowing the truths of the universe.

I clicked open the gate and walked up the path, first making sure that no one was near to see me, for I had a feeling of being watched, as though the house itself had eyes. There was a rustle in an overgrown bush that intruded on the path, and a large toad-like creature, the first I had seen on Priam, waddled out in front of me and plopped towards the front door. It turned to face me and raised its head, almost by way of invitation.

Curiously enough, I seemed to pick up telepathically a voice from the toad saying, "Go on, try it. It's a good house. Enter it, and you can have the knowledge of Satan himself."

Then it had gone into the bushes again.

So when, as I say, I saw that the house was good to live in, and pleasant to look at, and a house with a secret to make me wise, I went boldly to the door and put the key in the lock. I twisted it with some difficulty and turned the handle of the door. It swung open easily, and I stared into a dark hall. There seemed to be no danger, but all the same I moved cautiously step by step.

I could see doors on the right and on the left, and I chose the right. The room was very dark owing to the shuttered window. I stood still, letting my eyes adjust to the darkness. Gradually I saw that the room was without furniture, and I was about to try my luck with the left-hand room when I noticed something in the middle of the floor. I bent down to examine it, and saw it was a book. That was all I could see, and all that I was likely to see in the darkened room.

I dared not try to read it in the hall, since anyone might come past and see the door open. But I took one glance at the cover of the book before locking the door and taking the book home. There was a single word on the cover: SECRET. This was what I wanted.

Once I was home, I was in no hurry to open the book, but made myself a pot of tea and sat down in my favourite armchair to savour, as it were, the contents before I saw them, as though I were enjoying the smell of dinner before it came to the table.

Here in my hands I might be holding the deep secrets of the universe that Satan himself knew. With these secrets within my grasp I could be more powerful than any magician. I had heard that a magician could bind spirits to do his will. Might it even be that I could bind Satan to my will? I was intoxicated with the thought of power.

For one moment there flashed into my mind the story of the Sorcerer's Apprentice, who had looked into his master's book and enslaved a broom to carry buckets of water from the pool, only to end by nearly drowning himself in the flood that he was unable to stop. But that was only a story, and it certainly didn't apply to me.

I finished my cup of tea quite leisurely before placing the book carefully on the table. I was ready to open it and read it. I turned back to the cover, and read the title page again: SECRET.

Then I turned over to find Chapter One, and a mass of words met my eyes on the first page. But before I could read them they faded away and the page was blank. I turned over, and the words on the next pages vanished before my eyes. I became desperate, and flicked over a dozen leaves, only to be left with blank after blank where immediately before there had been words.

Was it the light that was the trouble? I switched on the electric light, but the words faded as quickly as before. I thought of the red light used in photography back on earth, and remembered a sheet of thin red plastic in one of the cupboards. I wrapped it round the electric bulb, and once more turned the pages, but the result was the same. And I noticed a strange thing. By mistake, I opened the book again at page one. There were the words once more from top to bottom of the page, but they faded as quickly as before. I closed the book in despair.

Now something unexpected happened. I had not read a single word in the book, and yet for a moment I knew everything in it. It is impossible to describe how and what I knew. I will not compare it to certain spiritual experiences, because these are often bound up with God-realisation, and God was not in what I knew in that moment of time.

I saw, not intellectually but experientially, the universe as a living body — with myself as an integral cell. The whole sensation was of an intense oneness, with a force of life upholding everything in one. And I was one with everything. In a flash I saw how a cell which was part of the whole could affect the whole by being part of the one life.

Thus I saw how Satan had been able to manipulate the forces of life for his own advantage. He was one dominant cell in the life of the universe. I too stretched out to dominate the whole, but in that moment the vision vanished. I fought to recapture it, but all that was left was an intellectual effort to describe what I had known in my heart for a few seconds to be the one life of the world, my life and everybody's life, the life of animal, plant and mineral. To describe it now makes it sound ridiculous, and yet I had known it.

The book still lay on the table. I looked at my watch. It was five o'clock, the time when each day my telepathic faculty was opened by Satan so that he could talk to me and listen to my spoken report and requests. I felt the semi-trance state coming over me, but I was afraid. I rose from my chair, and walked noisily across the room, singing the first song that came into my head. In this way, I hoped to hide, but the pressure of the inner voice continued.

"Where are you?" it called.

It was no use resisting, and I yielded. "I realised my own weakness, and I was afraid to meet you."

"You have not realised your weakness before. Why now? Have you been into the forbidden book?"

"I thought there was something there that I, as your servant, ought to know."

"So you didn't trust me. I had big plans for you, John. That house would have been yours, and I would have taught you from the book as much as it was good for you to know. But not now, not now. I believe you had a vision of what might have been, but that is all. You will not have that vision again."

The voice ceased, and the book was no longer on the table.

The key hung on the wall once more.

CHAPTER 11

I've already said that people commonly blame Satan for everything bad, and imagine that he is delighted with evil. I suppose that I also was influenced by this idea, and was anticipating an outburst of crime in our village. But Satan had assured me that his concern was to establish a community that would flourish without ever introducing the concept of God. To this end, he had no time for anything that would disrupt his community, and would take steps to control it.

Shortly after my experience at Secretum, we had our first disturbance. I was woken up soon after six-thirty by a hammering on the door. Dave Sugden, the storekeeper, stood on the doorstep, calling breathlessly, "We've been robbed!"

"Come in," I said, "while I put some clothes on. Your wife's all right, I take it."

"Yes, she's okay. She's staying at the shop. We've searched the place, and there's no one there now."

We went together. There was not much disturbance in

the shop, but a broken window showed how someone had come in and out. The till had been emptied, and all the tokens taken. Sugden and his wife had no idea how many tokens had gone. They had become so used to the quiet of the community that they had not bothered to keep count.

Sugden pointed to an empty space on one shelf where both of them remembered having stacked tins of food the previous day. They also thought that some cans of drink had gone. None of the tins or cans could easily be identified, since many households had stocked their larders, and the thief could claim that the things he had taken were part of the stock he and his family had paid for with their tokens.

Obviously the thief must be found. We had no policeman or detective in our number. We must be our own Sherlock Holmes. So I called our council together. This council had been elected since the initial general meeting. There were six of us, including Dr Faber and myself. The other four were Dave Sugden the storekeeper, Jim Token the farmer, Bill Broadwood the plumber, and Margaret Penny the wife of Joe Penny the printer.

We began going through the names of everyone in the village, men, women and even children, after agreeing that any comments or suspicions that any of us might express were privileged, and would not be repeated outside. After three hours we were no nearer a solution, and indeed we could not even make a list of suspects.

"Well", I said, "what can we do now? None of us knows how to take and judge fingerprints, even if there are any."

While I was talking, I felt my hand picking up my pen

from the table and moving rapidly over the pad of paper. I was sitting at a table, while the others were in easy chairs round the room, so they couldn't see what I had written. I glanced down and read, *Sam Smagle.*

I knew him as a rather morose bachelor who was working with our farmer in the fields. We had considered him among the list of names, but had dismissed him as too mild a man to commit a burglary. But the appearance of his name by automatic writing was surely more than a hint from "headquarters".

It had taken me several days to recover from the humiliation I had suffered at Secretum, but I was now myself again. Indeed, I took this information as a sign that I was once more in Satan's good books. I determined to make the most of it, and to take the credit for myself, and emphasise my authority.

"Then we've done all we can for the time being", I said. "If any of us discovers anything relevant, we will naturally follow it up. In the meantime this meeting is closed."

I tore the top sheet from the pad and pocketed it. The most sensible thing seemed to be to try a direct attack on Sam Smagle when he returned from his work in the fields.

I gave him time to have his tea before I knocked on his door. He seemed surprised to see me. I put my hand out, but he ignored it, and I could see that two of his fingers were bandaged.

"Have you cut your hand?" I asked.

He gave a grunt. "I cut it on a knife at the farm."

He stood aside for me. I had a quick look round the

living room, but naturally there was no sign of any cans or tins. I came straight to the point. "I am told you were out late last night."

"What if I was? It's none of your business."

"I thought you might help us with our enquiries into the burglary at the stores."

"How do you mean?"

"Well, did you see anyone about when you were out?"

"Can't say I did."

"Were you near the stores?"

He hesitated before replying, and I guessed he was thinking whether Yes or No would be the safer answer. "Yes" might lead to more detailed questions, but since I had led him to believe that someone had seen him, this might have been by the stores, and "No" would show him to be a liar.

So he replied, "I may have been. I was just wandering round. I couldn't sleep."

We were getting nowhere. I felt my position was sufficiently strong to accuse him directly. There would be no nonsense of libel, and in any case there was no witness present.

"Mr Smagle," I said, "you were seen breaking into the stores, and I suspect that you cut your fingers on the window glass. If I were to search your kitchen, I have no doubt at all that I would find the cans and tins you stole."

"Cans and tins are no proof. I've bought a lot and put them by. I've saved up my tokens too."

"Who has said anything about tokens?"

"Well, I assumed that whoever did it must have taken

money as well."

"Not good enough," I said. "You must meet the council and answer our questions."

We met next morning, and Sam Smagle was present. There was one piece of tangible evidence that forced him to confess. One of his fingers had become badly swollen, and he had to see the doctor. The trouble was a small piece of glass embedded in the cut.

He was willing to hand back everything to the stores, and we asked him to retire while we discussed what to do with him. There was not much that we could do except fine him, and we fixed the fine at fifty tokens, which we reckoned would more than cover the cost of a new shop window — if the glass could be teleported. I was delighted with the congratulations of the council on my cleverness in spotting the villain.

It wasn't much more than a week later that a major tragedy struck our community. Bill Stuckey, a married man without children, disappeared. He was one of the two electricians who worked at the turbine station. His wife Joan came to my house early one morning to say that he had not come home from his work on the previous evening, and there was no sign of him this morning. She said he often took a walk on his own in the evening, but was never out late.

We organised a search party, but there was no sign of Bill. No one remembered seeing him on his way home, and his wife couldn't say whether he had any favourite spot where he might have gone, and been taken ill.

We called off the search party before lunch, with the

idea of going out again in the afternoon. I was tired after my meal, and sank back in my large armchair to snatch a few minutes' sleep. Just as I was dozing off, I heard a voice, more strident than the telepathic communications which came from Satan:

"The pool before the lake."

Sleep vanished. Here was another chance to emerge as the great detective. There were a few men standing about in the street, and I called them to come with me for a fresh search. I suggested that we should take a walk to the stream and the lake just outside the village.

We struck the stream about a hundred yards from the lake, and walked slowly along it, looking into the water as we went. The water ran fairly swiftly until it was partially blocked by piles of brushwood which had floated down and become stuck at the exit from a pool. Here we stopped, and together we cleared some of the brushwood to let the water flow more freely.

"Look!" someone shouted.

We looked, and under the brushwood we saw first a pair of boots and then legs and a body. We were able to lean out over the water and grab the boots. Then we pulled the body of Bill Stuckey on to the bank. Someone took off a coat, and covered the swollen face.

In a moment of this kind one tends to panic, though I knew there was nothing one could do for Bill. But it was important not to act in a hurry and destroy any evidence there might be of accident, suicide or murder. I sent someone to fetch Dr Faber.

When he came, we stood back while he examined the

body. Then he called out, "Someone please help me turn him over."

The doctor's examination took a long time, but eventually he stood up. "That's all I can do now. I suggest someone fetches a stretcher from my surgery and some of you take him back there. His wife had better not see him yet, but someone must break the news to her. Does anyone know her well?"

One of the helpers, a near neighbour, volunteered that either he, or preferably his wife, would break the news to Joan.

"Have you any idea what happened, doctor?" he asked.

"Nothing you can tell Joan Stuckey yet. She need only know that he's been found drowned."

The neighbour went off, along with two others to fetch a stretcher from the surgery. The rest of us stayed behind with the doctor, who seemed reluctant to discuss the tragedy further. We chatted about this and that, rather than discussing the event that had brought us together. Then the stretcher came, and Dr Faber suggested taking the body to the shed at the bottom of his garden where he could if necessary make any further examination.

Bill's wife Joan apparently took the news quietly, and made no request to see the body.

CHAPTER 12

It was getting dark when there came a knock on my door. I opened it to find Dr Faber on the doorstep. "May I come in and have a word with you?" he asked.

Just as an aside, I wanted to keep the relationship between doctor and patient formal, which is why I usually refer to Peter Faber as the doctor, or Dr Faber. It's just something from my past that seems right.

I had a cup of coffee on the table, and poured another for the doctor. "I imagine it's something about Bill," I said.

"You're right. May I ask you a straight question? I'm told you said you knew where to find him, and led the others straight to the spot."

"It wasn't as definite as that. As far as I remember, I simply said I had an idea for a possible place to look for him."

"But you went straight there."

"Yes, I suppose I did. It was quite likely that he'd drowned himself, since we hadn't been able to find him anywhere else."

"You say he'd drowned himself."

"Or fallen in."

"Would you be surprised to find he'd been knocked out, maybe killed, by a blow on the back of the head before being pushed into the water?"

"Is that what you found when you examined him?"

"That is so. And, as we are alone, I must ask you again how you knew where to find him."

I suddenly realised what the doctor was thinking. "You're not suggesting I killed him?"

"I make no accusation. I am only warning you that you're bound to be under suspicion."

"If you can find a motive, you're cleverer than I am. I hardly knew the man."

"I'm sure you're right. I wouldn't suspect you, but others might. Perhaps we should meet as a council tomorrow morning."

"I'll call round on the members now. I take it that you haven't told anyone else yet that Bill was murdered."

"You're the only one who knows. It will come as a shock to the council tomorrow, I'm afraid."

He stood up, and I showed him to the door. When he had gone, I started on my round to the members of the council, and asked them to come for an informal inquest in the morning. Our lack of modern technology meant that we did not even have phones, a technology that in one form or another had been around for well over a hundred years. To use phones, there would need to be a central telephone exchange. I can honestly say that this was the first time I missed devices I had taken so much for granted back home.

When I was back in my house, I slumped down in the armchair, angry with Satan. He had told me where to go, and now he had trapped me. I could see I would be a suspect, once it was known that Bill had been murdered, since it was already being talked about that I had known where to find the body. I guessed that Satan was having his revenge for what I had done at Secretum. My only hope would be if Satan named the real murderer.

I tried to relax, but my mind was racing, and as long as this happened it was unlikely that I could contact Satan. I even called out, "Satan, tell me the murderer!" but there was no answer. I picked up a pen and put a sheet of paper on the table, and sat down in front of it. But nothing happened, no automatic writing.

When I went to bed, I struggled to get to sleep. But I must have slept for a second or two, because I had the flash of a vivid dream. I was by the water again, watching Bill being dragged to the bank. I distinctly heard a woman's voice say, "Ask Kathleen Ryecroft."

The voice was that of a young woman, which had broken through into my dream — clairaudience, but not clairvoyance, since I had not seen any woman in my dream of the river bank. I roused myself and wrote the name down, because dreams have a way of fading from memory by morning.

It was early morning when I woke again. The paper was there, and I had not written anything further in my sleep, only, *Ask Kathleen Ryecroft*. I knew her as the librarian in charge of the small library. She seemed a sensible enough girl, who in fact lived next door to the Stuckeys with her widowed father. I remembered that I had experienced a little hesitation when she and her father had answered the original advertisement.

Satan had warned me not to encourage anyone who, he said, might make trouble in the community. A widower and an unattached girl might cause the sort of trouble that Satan had in mind, but I judged the two were sensible enough for me to take the risk and accept them. Besides, they would be useful.

Peter Ryecroft was a shoemaker and cobbler, and worked in a well equipped shed at the bottom of his garden. He had requested what he needed for his trade, and the things had been brought. During the days that followed our arrival, I had begun to see what Satan had in mind over what he would provide. Tools, yes. Articles that *could* be made, but only if it was not possible for us to make them at present. So when someone asked for new shoes, they might be provided through the shop, or the person might be told to take the old shoes to Peter Ryecroft for repair. In this way Peter Ryecroft was building up quite a nice little business, as were other craftsmen also.

I had met his daughter Kathleen several times setting out for long walks in the country. She was by way of being a naturalist, and she told me that she was trying to list the plants, animals and birds which of course were often totally different from those on earth. Why I should be told to ask her about the death of Bill I couldn't say. But I decided to trust the dream voice.

I smiled as I thought I might after all score off Satan.

He had helped me to develop my psychic powers, and now, when he wouldn't give me the name of the murderer, I was on the way to finding it for myself by picking up what could have been a suggestion from the mind of someone who knew the murderer.

I called at the house soon after breakfast. Kathleen Ryecroft opened the door, and told me her father was in his workshop.

"Thank you," I said, "but I'd like to see you first."

She led me into the lounge and motioned me to sit down in one armchair, while she sat on the edge of the other. In what followed I couldn't help noticing that she had changed from the enthusiastic nature lover that I had met before, to a tight and restrained young woman.

"Well?" she asked.

"How well did you know Bill Stuckey?"

"Bill? My father Peter and I both knew him. He lived next door."

"I'm asking you, not your father."

"You'd better ask him."

"So I will, but I've found that a woman often notices more than a man. So I'm asking you."

"Notices what?"

"In your case, anything that might throw light on his death."

"How should I know?"

"Had he any enemies that you know of?"

"You mean, you think I know who killed him?"

I took her up. "You say 'Killed him'. Surely he was drowned, wasn't he? That means suicide or accident."

She didn't seem in the least perturbed. "You said 'enemies' so I thought you must mean something different from suicide or accident."

"Well, I did. Would you be surprised if I told you that he was killed before he was pushed into the water?"

Her face flushed red. "How was he killed? Do you know?"

"I know, Miss Ryecroft. I think you know too."

I was taking a chance, but I saw at once I had succeeded. Her face changed from red to pale. She stood up and went to the door.

"You said you'd be seeing my father," she said. "If you go out of the back door, you'll find him in his workshop now."

"You haven't answered my question," I insisted.

"What question? I don't remember you asking me one. If I remember, you merely expressed an opinion."

Before I had time to say anything, Kathleen had gone, shutting the door behind her.

I decided not to see her father just then, but he decided to see me. I had not been back home for more than a few minutes when he knocked violently on my door. When I opened it, Peter Ryecroft pushed his way inside.

His face was flushed, and he shouted at me, "My girl Kathleen tells me you've been pestering her. Anyone who pesters my girl won't get away with it — and there are some of those here."

"I'm sorry, Mr Ryecroft. I only asked her a few questions about your neighbour who's dead. Has someone been pestering your daughter?"

He cooled down somewhat.

"Pestering her!" he repeated. "You'd be surprised."

"I think I ought to know. I'm partly responsible for what goes on in the village."

"Thank you, I can deal with him in my own way. Anyway, you can stop bothering my girl with questions."

"I'm afraid I can't. The council is meeting shortly to investigate Bill Stuckey's death, and we'll need to ask your daughter Kathleen to tell us anything you know about him that might throw light on how he came to die in the pool."

"There's nothing we can tell you."

"Maybe not, but we'd like you both to come, as neighbours. You never know what may come out."

He hesitated for a moment before saying grudgingly, "Well, if you say so, you're the boss. We'll come — only don't expect us to say anything."

As he left, I said, "Eleven o'clock."

CHAPTER 13

I will not attempt to give a verbatim report of questions and answers at our council. Dr Faber began by telling us what he had already told me, that Bill Stuckey was knocked out and probably killed by a blow from some object like a heavy stone on the back of the head, before being thrown into the water.

I suggested that we should question any possible witnesses separately rather than have them together in the room. In particular, I impressed on the others that at this stage we should not disclose that Bill had been murdered, but continue to speak as though we were investigating a straightforward case of drowning.

I suggested that Joan Stuckey, Bill's wife, should be asked to come first. We were naturally apologetic about asking her questions, but she was perfectly self-possessed and dry-eyed.

In answer to our questions, she said she was not aware of anything troubling her husband. He had never threatened to take his life, and she assumed that he must have fallen into the water, perhaps after being taken suddenly ill. He was able to swim, so he must have been unconscious when he fell in.

Peter Ryecroft came in reluctantly after Joan Stuckey had left. I told him that we wanted to ask him a few questions about Bill.

"You mean Bill Stuckey? I imagine you didn't get anything useful from his wife."

"Joan was certainly helpful. Now we want to ask you a few questions. Often men notice things that a wife doesn't mention."

"Such as?"

"Well, was there any domestic trouble that might have upset Bill Stuckey?"

"Joan Stuckey would be the one to answer that. She was the one who lived with him!"

"So there's nothing you can add?"

I thought I detected some uneasiness. For some reason I felt prompted to ask a question for which I had no evidence.

"Mr Ryecroft, were you down by the river yesterday afternoon?"

He jumped up from his chair. "Did Joan Stuckey say that?" he asked angrily. "If she's trying to put the blame on me, I can tell you something about her. She hated him, I tell you."

He was walking up and down the room.

"Yes, he was a cruel man, knocking her about and abusing her. He deserved all he got."

"What are you talking about?" put in Susan Digby, a

rather formidable woman in her late fifties. I had chosen her for the trip because she seemed a sensible and reliable sort who could apply commonsense when necessary.

"She's making out I killed him, that's what you're all talking about, isn't it?" he shouted.

It was Dr Faber who answered. "We're investigating the case of a man found drowned. You're speaking as though someone was to be blamed for his death. Have you any reason for suggesting this?"

Peter Ryecroft stopped walking, and stared at us before answering hesitatingly. "I didn't say anyone ... killed him. I just thought you wouldn't be making such a song and dance unless you suspected something. And if so, I don't want to be the person suspected."

I guessed he would probably now be on his guard, and we would get nothing more out of him at present. So I asked him to send his daughter Kathleen in, but to be ready to come back if we wanted him to help us further.

Kathleen Ryecroft was obviously uneasy, but sat down ready to answer our questions. I began by saying that her father had admitted being by the river during the afternoon. She nodded. I asked whether she knew if anyone was with him. Her reaction took us by surprise. She spoke up loudly. "Yes. He was with that woman."

"Do you mean Joan Stuckey?"

"Who else? My father was in and out of Joan's house all the time when her husband Bill was out working up at the turbine. Or else she was in with us — only not so often, because I could see what was going on."

Susan Digby spoke again. "Kathleen, that's a very serious thing to say. Didn't the neighbours talk?"

"No. Our houses are next to each other, and there's a gap in the fence at the back. There's a hedge between us and the road, so people can't see in. It was all very private."

Susan pressed her. "But you said they were together by the river yesterday."

"They must have gone out separately. But I saw them together by the river."

By now Kathleen was obviously prepared to talk, and it became clear that she blamed her father as much as "that woman". It transpired that her father had carried on secretly with other women even while her mother was alive. Yet he was continually suspicious of her, and of any men she knew, even though she was now getting on for thirty.

I told Kathleen that her father had spoken of men pestering her. I apologised for asking, but was anyone pestering her now?

"I suppose that's a fair question in the circumstances. Yes, Bill Stuckey was continually making suggestions, but I can assure you there was nothing on my side. To be honest, I'm not interested in sex. Sex is the body, and the body is a bar to higher things. I was doing my best to stop him for good."

I detected a gasp from the council members.

Kathleen blushed. "That sounds bad, but I didn't kill him. That isn't what I meant. He was always pressing me to meet him, and I agreed to see him by the river on his way back from work at the electricity station. I can see now I was stupid, and that he would put a wrong construction on my fixing a quiet place, but I honestly intended to have it out with him once and for all, and I couldn't do it at my home or his, without my dad or Joan Stuckey knowing." She paused.

"So what happened?" asked the doctor.

"I met him, and he suggested we should sit on the bank together. We sat above the pool, and I told him that nothing he could say or do would persuade me. He put his arm round me, and I sprang up and rushed away. I glanced over my shoulder, and he was sitting staring across the pool. He called, 'All right, Kathleen. I know you love me, and I'll wait for you to come back.' Then I heard someone coming, and I crouched down in the bushes.

"I couldn't see him now, but I was still near enough to hear him say, 'So you've come back, Kathleen', and a voice replied 'Not Kathleen. It's Joan.' I heard a thud, and crept out. That woman and my father were bending over Bill. My dad said, 'Help me throw him in, and throw that stone in too.' Then there was a splash, and I ran away."

She broke down and wiped her eyes with her handkerchief. I asked one more question.

"Did you see which of them had the stone?"

"No. By the time I looked, they were both pushing the body into the water."

We thanked her, and I showed her into another room so that she should not meet her father.

We were not a court of law, or even a jury, but we believed we were competent to reach a decision in the light of what we had heard. Kathleen Ryecroft's story rang true, especially since she had not known that the post mortem showed that Bill Stuckey had been first knocked unconscious. Peter Ryecroft had shown that he knew he had been murdered, and had implied that Bill's wife had as much right to be accused as he had. Admittedly she had not said anything significant when we questioned her, but she had the right to be told what we now believed to be the case.

So we asked her to come back, and told her that evidence showed that her husband had been knocked unconscious by a blow on the back of the head before being thrown into the water. She gave what was obviously a pretence of being surprised, and her cheeks flushed red. We told her we had evidence that she was by the pool about the time of the murder, and her reaction was the same as Peter's had been. She exploded in a hysterical attack on Peter.

"He told you, did he? He wanted my Bill out of the way. It was his idea we should meet him there on his way back from work and do him in."

On the evidence, we decided unanimously that in effect both were equally guilty. But we were at a loss to know what to do with them. We had no prison, and none of us wanted to put them to death. We had to allow them to return home and let the rumour get out that they had murdered Bill Stuckey. Would their only punishment be a boycott by their neighbours?

I was naturally anxious to have a response from Satan himself.

On my next talk with Satan, he congratulated me on the way we had handled the case. I asked how the two should be punished, or should we show them mercy.

"No mercy. They've degraded our community."

"But they are people," I pointed out, "and surely individuals must be treated as individuals."

"You know very well that I set apart this community to show that a community can be prosperous without a belief in an alleged god. Murder wrecks a community, and murderers must be removed."

Satan removed them that night, and we saw them no more. I don't know how Satan managed it, but everyone seemed to accept their disappearance. No search party went out, and their names seemed to be quickly forgotten. Even Kathleen didn't question what had happened to her father. It was as though memories had been wiped, or questioning blocked.

The Stuckeys' house remained empty, and Kathleen continued living in her father's house next door, where she had been housekeeper to her father for many years on earth.

When I met her, I was surprised to find how calm she seemed. I think she had come to hate her father for his carryings-on with other women, and for his domination of her in the home. Although she didn't say it, I sensed her relief that he was here no more.

CHAPTER 14

I had no idea that I would have such trouble over the disposal of Bill Stuckey's body. "Disposal of the body" is calling a spade a spade, but disposal it was to me. I had my first surprise when I called to see Dr Faber, and asked him to suggest a couple of men who would dig a grave somewhere outside the village, and help me to take Bill's body there after dark.

The doctor and Sarah his wife were together, and both looked surprised. He spoke first. "My dear man, you can't bury him without a proper funeral."

She nodded, and added, "The people would never forgive you."

I shook my head vigorously. "I don't intend to be party to a superstitious religious hangover."

"Why should it be religious?" the doctor asked.

"Have you ever known a funeral that didn't bring God in somewhere?" his wife put in.

"You can give a funeral address without mentioning God," I insisted. "This is worse and worse. First you expect me to have a funeral, and now you say I have to give an address."

The doctor nodded. "I think you told me you read classics at university. You probably read the funeral speech by Pericles on the Athenians who fell in the war. He never mentioned God, and it was a good address."

"Ah," I said, "Pericles was praising heroes, and exalting the good sides of Athenian life. I can't see Bill Stuckey fitting that picture."

"Yes, I see what you mean. But you can say something about survival, without being religious."

Thereupon we embarked on an argument about survival. Peter Faber maintained that survival, or even the immortality of the soul, had no connection with God. He quoted two examples of patients who seemed to have died on the operating table, but who came round with similar stories of having left their bodies and observed all that was going on from up above, and then had passed through a tunnel and had seen relatives who had died. They were then drawn back into their bodies. They had not seen God, nor were they religious before or after, although they had come to believe in life after death. They felt that their short experience out of the body might well be extended after dying.

The doctor went on to say he had been sufficiently interested to look for further evidence, and he and his wife had read a fair amount of spiritualistic writings. They had become confirmed in their belief that such evidence as there was, did not involve a belief in God.

"Mediums are good and kind people," he added.

"What about fakes?" I asked.

"Oh yes, there have been some who have traded on human grief, or on the desire to find evidence of survival. But there are plenty who are honest. My point is that down the centuries, since the days of Moses, and probably before, spiritualism has produced no proof of the existence of God. No, I think even a humanist can be glad of the messages from the mediums. They tell us to be good boys and girls, and be assured that life will go on much the same as before. If the mediums are religious, they may describe themselves as Christians, but their god is very much an impersonal force, and Christ is an inspired teacher, but not God. I agree with that."

He paused for breath.

I said, "If you are even partly convinced, you must have formed some theory of where the dead are, and what they are doing."

The doctor replied, "I can't say where they are. I'm inclined to think most of them are existing in a subjective world of their own, a kind of intelligent dreaming. So they may develop ideas that are an extension of what they held on earth. Lesser spirits continue the social life as before, dreaming their smokes and drinks into subjective reality. If you could get Bill Stuckey to communicate, you'd probably find he'd picked up a subjective girl in the beyond."

I didn't know if he was serious about Bill, but the doctor had started a new train of thought. I began to see that a good speech at the interment might well help our cause.

Almost all the community turned up for the funeral. I felt a kind of inspiration laying hold of me as I spoke sympathetically of the one we were laying to rest. Admittedly the phrase "laying to rest" was traditional, but I could not think of a better. Even if Bill Stuckey had not been all he should have been, this was no excuse for the murderers. We must all strive to learn from the errors and mistakes of others.

None of us believed that Bill Stuckey would have to go before an angry God in the skies, but there was no reason to believe that part of him had not survived, and he might be learning from his mistakes. We could wish him well. On the other hand there might be no survival, and in that case there was nothing more to say.

We lowered Bill Stuckey into the grave, and I recited the words, "Earth to earth, ashes to ashes, dust to dust," and turned away to leave the others to cluster round the open grave. Kathleen Ryecroft was there. She held no handkerchief to her eyes. She was completely composed.

No one asked what had become of her father and Joan Stuckey.

That evening I saw Dr Faber and his wife again. I felt vaguely uneasy, in case somehow religion was trying to get in among us by the back door. But the doctor was again insistent that it was sensible to accept survival without having to believe in God. He said that he could not feel that his essential self could ever cease to exist, yet he didn't believe in God. Moreover, he didn't like to think that all he had tried to do as a doctor, which in a sense was part of himself, could be wasted in nothingness. He couldn't put it into words, but it meant a lot to him.

Then he turned an argument on me. "You've told me

you and your boss are trying to demonstrate that a community can flourish without God. Who are you going to demonstrate it to? Are we all going to be taken back to earth to show what good boys and girls we are? Or is your boss the only one who will see the results?"

I told him to be patient.

The doctor shook his head. "So far as I can see, we'll all go one by one, and in a hundred years there won't be many children and children's children left to see the results. But if we all pass on, and meet people from earth again, we'll be able to demonstrate what we've done. So your demonstration, if it means anything, must mean survival."

"Survival for ever and ever?" I asked.

"Who can say? In the end we may just fade out in the beyond. That may seem to contradict what I've said, but I don't think it does. Our thoughts and feelings take us so far, but we're going to need a revelation now to take us further."

I went home with my thoughts going round and round. I picked up a sheet of paper and a pencil. While I looked at the clock to see the time, my hand wrote, *A good speech. Stick to realities, and leave religious faith alone.*

CHAPTER 15

Shortly after this, I was puzzled by a strange message from Satan. He told me to go to the centre of the wood where I would meet one of his servants. I've already described my visit to the edge of that dark wood, how I somehow disliked it, and I had not been since. Yet I had kept telling myself that I would go back one day, and now it seemed I would have to go, whether I wanted to or not.

The sun shone as I started out, with blue sky, like late spring in England. Flowers covered the banks on each side of me, as I followed the path to the wood. At first the trees were few, but gradually they became more crowded and the branches began to close overhead. Now I was surrounded by thick shrubs, twice my height, pressing in on me. At times I had to push them aside to get through.

All I could follow were the marks of a track. How it came to be there, I couldn't tell. Maybe animals regularly passed that way, and indeed several times I heard rustlings in the bushes, and once the crashing of some larger animal running away from me.

Presently I heard the chattering of water. The ground began to slope to the left, and I came to a gully across the track, with a stream and small waterfall running down it. The track led to a piece of rock, with another rock on the other side. If I wanted to go down to cross the stream, I would have to climb down a steep and slippery bank, with an equally steep bank to climb on the other side, so I decided I would jump across from rock to rock.

I suppose the distance was no more than four feet, an easy distance if I kept my head, but I admit I stared at the gap for two or three minutes before plucking up my courage to take a running jump. It turned out to be easier than I had thought, and I continued to follow the track on the other side.

I had no idea how far I had to go. Satan had said the centre of the wood, and I assumed that I would be given some sign when I got there. I was not mistaken.

The track suddenly ran out in a clearing. A circle of trees stood back, letting the bright sun come slanting in. To my fancy they seemed like a ring of giants, waiting to watch what would happen.

As my eyes became used to the brightness after the gloom of the wood, I saw a large fallen tree lying across the grass. And on the log sat a girl, dressed in dark blue, with her hair hanging down over her face. I stopped still, and stared. So this was Satan's servant, whom he said I must meet. As I watched, she tossed her head back so as to throw her hair off her face. I gasped, it was Kathleen Ryecroft, and she was staring at me.

I was angry, very angry. Satan had been deceiving me

all along. He had given me to understand that I was to be his agent, the only agent on Priam. And now there was this young woman whom he wanted me to meet as his servant. Who knows what he had been doing through her without my knowing!

I was in two minds whether to turn back, but since this person was evidently my rival I didn't care to risk losing such influence as I still had. So I walked slowly forward.

Kathleen jumped off the trunk and walked to meet me, with a smile on her face. "I'm glad you've come," she said. "Oh, I'm so glad. I've been terribly scared. I willed you to come, and now you're here."

Her words took me by surprise. This didn't sound like Satan's servant.

"How do you mean you willed me?" I replied.

"Oh, come off it. Don't pretend you don't know we're both psychic."

"Should I have known?"

She repeated solemnly the words I had heard in my dream. *"Ask Kathleen Ryecroft."*

"So it was your voice."

"Of course it was. It was one of the few occasions when I've travelled out of my body at night."

"You mean astral projection."

"I found myself in your house and I sensed your restlessness, although I didn't go up to your bedroom. You seemed to be asking, 'Who was it?' over and over again. So I answered, 'Ask Kathleen Ryecroft', and you heard me."

"So that's what happened. You seem all right now, but you said a moment ago you were scared."

Her face changed. "Yes, I need someone here with me, and as you heard me once, I thought you might hear me again."

"So I'm here. What can I do? Tell me."

"I was exploring in the wood. I'm keen on birds and flowers as you know. Then suddenly I felt terrible pressure in my head — not a headache or anything like that. It was somehow inward, as though I was being attacked, seized, possessed."

"Are you a medium?" I asked.

"No. Occasionally I'm clairvoyant, but not a medium. The funny thing is, I feel I might be going into a trance and I'd be terrified to pass out without anyone by me."

"You'd better rest. Come back and sit on the fallen tree again."

She said, "Sometimes I've been clairvoyant and I've seen pictures and heard voices coming from someone's mind. They seemed like someone coming back from the dead, but I knew they weren't. This is something different."

We sat in silence for a few seconds. Then she asked me to hold her hand. I had the same feeling as people have from time to time, of becoming aware of myself, almost as though I was somebody else watching. But if I was self-conscious, Kathleen was not. She closed her eyes, gave several deep breaths, and remained still.

Whether or not some power passed through my hand, and into her, I couldn't tell, but all of a sudden she jumped off the log. She seemed taller and grosser. Her expression was changing. If it had not been for her clothes, I would have sworn that a man was standing in front of me — Bill

Stuckey, back from the dead. And when Kathleen opened her mouth, it was Bill's voice that spoke.

"At last I've got you," the voice said. "All of you. You're mine now, though you wouldn't have me on earth. Mine for ever and ever."

I watched helplessly. When Kathleen sprang from the fallen tree, I had let go of her hand. A sense of horror gripped me as I realised what had happened. Kathleen was hopelessly possessed.

The word *exorcism* flashed into my mind, the casting out of the evil spirit of Bill from his victim. I couldn't use Christian exorcism, but my studies had led me to believe that a magician could set off one spirit against another, a stronger against a weaker. If Satan was the strongest spirit, he could surely conquer this one.

I held up my right hand and shouted, "In Satan's name, I command you to leave her alone."

Immediately Kathleen dropped to the ground and lay face downwards.

A man's voice from behind me, not Bill's, said, "She'll come round in a few minutes. Leave her alone. I have a message for you from my master."

I turned round, but there was no one in sight. Yet the voice continued from nearby.

"My master has a sense of humour. He told me to impersonate Bill, to see how you'd react. I think I did it very well."

"You certainly did," I replied bitterly. "And I did well too."

"Yes," said the voice. "I might have had the woman

longer, but you made me give her up. Now, before she comes round, listen to my message. This woman is psychic enough to have almost discovered our secret. If she finds it on her own, she'll talk about it, and my master's whole plan will be ruined. My master orders you to tell her as much as necessary, but first you must pledge her to secrecy. She may even help you. Indeed you may marry her if that seems best."

I suddenly saw my relation to Satan in a new light. I had thought I was his big man in command. Now he was treating me as a slave whose life had to be entirely directed by him to fit his plans.

"Tell your master," I said, "that I don't intend to marry, and I'll use *my* discretion about what to tell Kathleen Ryecroft. I'm happy enough single, and she told the council she's not interested in sex. So we'll stay as we are, thank you!"

"So be it," the voice replied, growing fainter.

There was a movement at my feet. Kathleen raised herself on her hands, and I helped her to get up.

"What happened?" she asked, as she looked around.

"A spirit came and claimed to be Bill, but he was an imposter, another sort of spirit."

She shuddered. "You mean I was possessed."

"Yes, I'm afraid so. But he's gone, and I don't think he'll come back."

"I'll resist him. I couldn't stand it again. In fact, I'll close my mind to clairvoyance and things like that for ever. Oh, I'm glad you were here."

She put her face up and kissed me on my cheek, and

stepped back blushing. "I'm so sorry. Whatever must you think of me? I can't think what made me do it. I've never kissed a man before, except my father."

"It was a kiss of gratitude," I answered.

"How very formal that sounds. But you're probably right." She looked away, and brushed herself down.

"Now listen," I said, "there's something I must tell you."

Kathleen looked at me again now, as I went on.

"I think you've guessed that the things that have happened aren't just what they seem."

"I've guessed that, but I can't get any further. I know it's more than a matter of psychic teleports."

I first bound Kathleen to secrecy between the two of us. Then I went back to the beginning, and told her all that had happened. I explained that Satan's purpose in forming this community was to demonstrate that men and women could enjoy a good life, and have a prosperous society, without worrying about God. I said that as long as they are on earth, people are always being influenced by ideas of God — here, Satan ruled absolutely.

"You mean Satan is our god now."

"Exactly. But no one else knows."

"Then why have you told me?"

"Because the message that came just now was that we are to work together."

"I see. As Satanists."

"That's an unpleasant word. We're helping a master with his plan."

"I've promised to keep it a secret, and I will. I can see now why may father was taken away, along with Joan

Stuckey. They didn't fit in with Satan's plans after their crime." She sighed. "Now I'm feeling tired and drained out. Let's get home."

Kathleen coiled up her hair, brushed herself down once more, and led the way from the patch of bright sunlight along the heavily overshadowed track. When we had jumped the stream, and had come to the edge of the wood, she told me to stay for a few minutes and then take a different way back.

"Otherwise I'll be getting a reputation, after what happened with Bill Stuckey. Everyone knows he tried to be intimate with me. And if you need to see me any time, catch me on my own in the library, or send me a message to come to your house after dark. So, goodbye for now."

"Goodbye!" I called after her, and sat down on the bank until I judged she had reached home.

CHAPTER 16

I had not anticipated that Christmas would produce a crisis. I'd not bothered with dates, but one or two had diaries with them, and knew we had come to December. We had been brought to a planet where the climate was equable all through the year, so there was no obvious change from autumn to winter.

The first indication I had of things to come was when a deputation of four, two men and two women, appeared at my door. I brought them in, and they lost no time in coming to the point.

"Some of us want to be taken back home for Christmas."

"I'm afraid that's impossible," I said.

One of them shouted back. I knew him as Harry Haskins, who in an amateurish way was trying to take on the cobbler's job now that Peter Ryecroft had gone.

"It's not impossible at all! You and your boss got us here, and you can get us back again."

The others murmured assent.

"I don't say we can't get you back to earth, but it's impossible to upset the plan that we all agreed to. Priam is to be our permanent home, and we will never settle if we want to go dashing across the galaxy."

"But we've always spent Christmas with relations," put in one of the women.

"I'm sorry, but from now onwards we will have Christmas together here."

"Is that your last word?" demanded Harry.

"It is."

Harry got up, and the others followed reluctantly. They all went out. I was rather worried about the affair, and was even more worried by a telepathic message from Satan a few days later. This concerned the weekly paper, a folder of four pages which our printer Joe Penny produced on the old machine with removable lead type, something that I had not seen in use for a long time until now.

Joe had wanted a modern offset printing machine, or a simple word processor and printer. Failing that, an old typewriter and a photocopier. But no, none of that technology was allowed on Priam. I had to remind everyone that we were living as though in a period of history when life was simple, because in spite of all its advances, science and technology had done little to promote peace.

I can see now that the failure to supply even something as basic as a typewriter was to do with security. Letters and notices had to be written by hand, which meant that all handwriting could be identified in the event of something subversive being written that might cause problems to Satan.

Joe Penny relied on contributions from any of us who sent anything in. In particular he was helped by Horace Humpole, who had gained some part-time experience as a journalist, and who produced a leading article each week, adapted in length to fit such space as needed filling.

The old press must have been a deliberate choice, to avoid Joe Penny being able to print too large a newspaper; for the more opportunity there was for the people to submit articles, there more opportunity there was for them to share their grievances with the whole village.

The message that came to me from Satan was that the paper would not be published the following morning, but I would be given a proof of an article that concerned him and myself. I must destroy this as soon as I had read it.

Next morning I was woken up by a loud banging on my front door. While I put on my dressing gown, the banging continued. On opening the door I found Joe Penny dancing with rage on the doorstep.

"What's happened to my papers?" he shouted at me.

"What *has* happened to them?" I asked.

"You know very well. You've taken them."

"I haven't even seen them," I replied, curious to know why I was being accused.

He grew calmer, and I asked again, "Joe, why do you think I'm responsible, if you mean they've been stolen?"

He hesitated before answering. "Didn't you know there was a leader about you and your boss?"

"No," I said, "but what if there was?"

"You didn't want anyone else to see it, so you stole it."

"You mean it was as bad as that. No, I didn't steal it. Anyway, why couldn't you print off some more copies?"

"I could have done, but whoever stole the copies broke up the typeface, and scattered the type all over the floor. All the letters are jumbled. It will take me a day or two to get them all sorted."

"I would like to express my sympathy, but if the article is an attack on me, I suppose I must be glad. Anyway, let me assure you I've no idea who took the papers."

"I'll find him all right," Joe Penny declared, as he let himself out of the house.

I understood more of the wisdom of Satan's choice of printing press, for it would take Joe and Horace too long to reset the pages for a reprint today.

On my return to my bedroom, I found a sheet of paper on my bed. It was a proof copy of the leading article. I cannot quote it exactly, since I obeyed orders and destroyed it after I had read it. It contained a series of attacks on me and my unknown boss, and as far as I can recollect it made the following complaints:

I was refusing a reasonable request to allow families to return home for Christmas. Since they had been brought here by unknown means, surely they could return with the same means. Why should John Longstone have control of their lives? He was no different from other people. Why should not the community elect another leader, and command Longstone to tell him all they wanted to know? There was far too much secrecy.

There didn't seem much that I could do, though I could see that I might soon have a revolt on my hands. Satan, however, kept me informed of what was going on. Horace Humpole, who had written the leader, was on the warpath and was calling a few sympathisers to a private meeting in his house.

Satan told me what happened at the meeting, although all who came were sworn to secrecy. I went out of my way to tackle Humpole first thing in the morning, and discussed the meeting with him, naming the chief speakers who had attacked me.

The same thing happened more than once. Whenever two or three started grumbling or agitating, I knew about it, and always took the chance of meeting them personally and showing how well I was aware of their conversation. I did this on my own responsibility without being prompted by Satan. I imagined that it would enhance my influence, and kill further ideas of revolt.

In fact, it had the opposite effect. One morning a notice appeared on the wall outside my house, scrawled with the words BIG BROTHER IS WATCHING YOU. Two days later another notice announced a reward for information about spies. Satan told me that Harry Haskins, the new cobbler, was responsible for much of the agitation, but warned me against doing anything more for now.

Satan's intimate knowledge of what was happening puzzled me. Until now, at the back of my mind I had held the popular assumption that, like the Christian concept of God, he was omnipresent. I had now realised that like any other being he could be in only one place at a time. I had seen more of him because I was at present at the centre of his plans, but even here he couldn't be dropping into all the houses simultaneously.

He had already told me that he had subordinates who had prepared Priam for us, and now I realised that other spirits, or perhaps the same ones, were keeping a watch on everyone and reporting back to their master.

Two days after the second notice had gone up, Satan told me that the time had come to assert my leadership. I must not doubt him, but must do everything he told me, however ridiculous it seemed.

The first thing I had to do was to announce a meeting of every man, woman and child, to be held on the village green the next evening. I was doubtful whether all would come, but so far as I could judge they were all there. I walked out among them without any idea of what I was supposed to do. I could only hope that Satan would open up our "hot line" and tell me.

The crowd drew back and stared grimly at me as I walked through. Then suddenly the tension was broken by a child calling out, "Mummy, I want my tea!" Another shouted, "I want mine too." One or two in the crowd smiled, but someone called to me, "Get on with it, can't you! Can't you see they're hungry?"

Now Satan's prompting came through, and I knew what to do. I picked up some stones and put them on the ground in front of me.

"Come here, children," I called. "I'll give you some tea. Would you like some buns? Then look! Here they are! Come and take them."

As I spoke, where once there had been stones, there now were buns. A child picked one of them up and bit a piece out of it. He turned to the others with his mouth full, and nodded.

"It's good," he managed to say.

The other children dived on them.

There was some applause from a few in the front, and those behind struggled to see for themselves. Several looked at me with awe, but someone, I think Haskins, called out, "It's only a trick. I've seen it on telly."

His words pricked the bubble. Others took it up. "It's a trick!" and one mother snatched the bun from her child, and stamped on it. Someone called out, "When's the next performance?"

I held up my hand for silence. I heard the well-known inner voice, "Tell them to watch this." I added something of my own as a feeling of exhilaration gripped me.

"If you don't believe my power to turn these stones into food, then watch."

To be honest, I had no idea what would happen next. But suddenly I felt myself slowly rising from the ground. The people fell back with exclamations of amazement. Up and up I went, until I was able to perch on the edge of the roof of a three storey house. There I stayed, as though suspended in the air.

The doctor's voice floated up to me, though whether he was airing his knowledge, or trying to calm the crowd's excitement, I can't say. "It's levitation. Other people have done it in the past. But it's clever."

It looked as though once again the demonstration of my

power would fall flat. Then the voice came, "Now jump down. Jump!"

I said, "I'll be smashed to pieces."

The voice spoke again. "I told you to trust me. I've given my servants orders to hold you up. You won't be hurt."

So I just jumped into space. For a moment I fell like a stone, and it flashed through my mind that this was Satan's way of killing me. But some six feet from the ground it was as though a parachute had opened, and I landed with no more force than if I had jumped a foot in the air.

The doctor seized me by the hand. "I've read about levitation before, about Joseph of Copertino and Daniel Douglas Home, and all that, but I'd no idea it could be done as you did it. Good psychic stuff. Congratulations!"

I doubt whether many understood what Dr Faber was talking about, but they evidently gained the impression that anyone could do the stunt if only they knew how the trick was done.

"What *is* the next trick?" someone shouted.

"That's all," I called.

There was some half-hearted clapping as the people dispersed.

Next morning another notice appeared. ASK THE CONJURER TO YOUR CHRISTMAS PARTY.

So Christmas was still an issue, but I kept making it clear that a return to earth was not on the cards. And although they had treated my display as an elaborate trick, for the time being they dropped their opposition. I couldn't forbid Christmas on Priam.

So in due course one or two brought a tree from the woods and set it up on the green. People requested various decorations and crackers, and hung them on the branches. On Christmas Day, although I stayed in my house the whole morning, I know they gave each other presents, and someone left an iced cake on my doorstep.

In the late afternoon a number gathered to dance round the tree. I had been afraid we might have carols, but like myself most were sufficiently pagan to have abandoned Christian hymns long ago. But they joined in some of the better known old music hall songs and a few from World War II.

I remembered my skill with my funeral sermon, and thought I might justify my position as leader with another suitable address on this occasion. So I stood on a small mound and clapped my hands for silence at a break in the singing.

I declared that we had gone behind the traditions that were kept up by many people on earth. We may still keep the meaningless name of Christmas, but we were observing the good old Yule customs that the world had celebrated from time immemorial. If we had been on earth, we would be joining our ancestors in rejoicing that we had come to the period when the sun, which had sunk to its lowest point, now began to increase in strength day by day. On Priam, where the seasons changed little, we could not perceive any change at this time, but we nonetheless accepted the invisible fact as a real event to be celebrated.

I didn't detect much enthusiasm for my speech. In fact the conclusion was somewhat spoilt by the appearance of

Santa Claus from the doctor's house, with packets of homemade sweets for the children.

Dr Faber received the applause that should have been mine.

CHAPTER 17

A week or two later I met Peter Faber outside my house, and walked along a little way with him. I asked him jokingly how was business at the surgery, and was surprised to find him answering seriously.

"It's a funny thing. For the first time I'm getting more than I should expect, considering our total numbers."

"What's the matter with them, Doctor? We haven't got an epidemic on our hands, have we?"

"Oh no, nothing like that. Quite a proportion of the troubles are what I would diagnose as psychosomatic. You know, of course, what that means."

"Of course. What unkind people call 'All in the mind', but a bit more than that, and quite real enough."

"I find I'm having to dish out more tranquilisers than I should like. I hadn't expected to do that in a place like this. To my mind, the peace of the place ought to be enough."

He looked all round him. We were clear of the houses by now. He went on. "We've had several small accidents too — a sprained ankle, a nasty burn, and a cut on the head through falling against the edge of a table. Ah well! I mustn't bore you with my troubles. After all, medical care is what I'm here for."

"That's true" I said, "but I hope you're happy in your work."

"I think so. But there's something about the atmosphere that depresses me and my wife at times. I can't put it into words, but somehow I feel as though we're in a prison camp, free to walk around, but with warders watching all the time. Funny how one's imagination can play tricks."

I thought it best not to pursue the subject in the light of what I knew, and we walked on, talking of things in general.

A bright golden bird flew across our path. The doctor pointed to it and told me that he was preparing a set of descriptions of birds, flowers and insects on Priam. He had always been interested in nature on earth, and had been pleased to find some of his nature books teleported in his bookcase here. I suggested he might get in touch with Kathleen Ryecroft the librarian, who also was doing nature research. He nodded, and continued talking.

"The trouble is thinking up new names for everything. At the moment I'm relating them to the nearest I can find in my books. Maybe I'll call that a golden oriole."

A loud whistle came from the tree where the bird had landed.

"Yes," nodded the doctor, "I once heard an oriole on the earth. That was just like it."

I think this was the day when I actually saw Satan again in person, for the first time since we had been on Priam. It was early evening, and as on the first occasion I suddenly became aware of a figure in the armchair opposite. He was dressed in black, as before.

He began, "I thought you'd prefer to have a talk face to face instead of our usual communications."

"Probably, yes," I said. "But it depends what you want to talk about."

"You may wish to ask me something."

"I'd sooner you said what you have to say first."

"Very well. You're not doing too badly on the whole."

"Thank you."

"I was sorry that our attempts to demonstrate your authority before Yuletide were such a failure. You recognised what I was doing, of course."

"I guessed you were trying the same plan as you used with Jesus, when you suggested turning stones into bread and throwing himself from the roof of the temple. It didn't work with him. He wouldn't do what you said."

"I'm sorry to have to admit it, but he was right and I was wrong. When *you* actually did it, my plan was a failure. I can see that the priests and others would not have been impressed by a man drifting down from the roof."

"I'm surprised you didn't foresee it."

"You seem to think I can foresee the future. I can work out quite a lot, and I can have occasional intuitions, but I cannot see the end from the beginning."

"Then, if I may say so, why did you worry about stopping Jesus, if you didn't know his plan?"

"Because he was driven by an obsessive idea that he was destined to die a violent death. He had read about it in a set of predictions in the Hebrew prophets."

"What did it matter to you?"

"I sensed that it did, and I was right. A whole lot of people, as you know, got hold of the idea that he was the God they had imagined existed — and that was the start of all the trouble that I've been fighting ever since."

I saw the point, but added, "What about the other suggestion that you made to Jesus, to become ruler of the world by acknowledging you as lord? You didn't try that with me."

Satan laughed. "No. You tried to get that for yourself in the house of secrets. You've been getting too big for your boots. Your place is under me, not living as my partner."

He leaned back in his chair, with a wave of his hand to brush the subject away. Then he went on, "The doctor's been telling you of his accident cases, hasn't he? Did it strike you I might be responsible?"

"What do you mean?"

"As a former theologian, you know that Christians talk as though their God punishes what they call sin. I've often heard them say, 'What have I done to deserve this?' But of course things don't work out according to their theory."

I nodded agreement.

"Well, I'm more consistent. Every one of those accidents was a punishment to nip trouble in the bud. One man was starting to knock his wife about, another was drunk, and the woman was persistently nagging her husband and threatening to take up with another man."

"Then how could you cause the accidents?"

"A moment's mental confusion. The result, a trip over

the edge of the carpet, a fall against the table, or a dropped saucepan of boiling water. You can take it from me, they all feel guilty now."

Again Satan dismissed the subject, and surprised me by asking, "What about Kathleen Ryecroft these days? You've not seen much of her since that time in the wood."

That was true. I had done little more than say good morning when I met her out, and we exchanged what I suppose would be called "significant glances" when I went to change a book at the library. But we had not gone out of our way to seek each other out.

"You will put me in a difficult position", I said, "if you're suggesting I should marry her. I've no intention of marrying, and Kathleen once hinted to the council that she felt the same."

"That's all very well, but she's put *me* in a difficult position. She was psychic enough to be on the verge of guessing what was happening, and now you've had to tell her of my plan. She may very well try some unfortunate experiment on her own. That's why it would be best to marry her, so that you could keep an eye on her."

I know my face showed resentment. "You can't make me marry her."

"I can only advise you for the good of the cause which you and I have undertaken. I'm prompting her to meet you in half an hour by the lake. She's on her way now. If she passes the spot where she saw Bill Stuckey murdered, a little bit of extra emotion won't do her any harm. Don't be late!"

The armchair was empty. I could see no dent in the

cushion. It was the first time I had been angry with my boss, but my mind was raging as I went down the street. I also began to think just how much he could influence my mind. I knew the feeling of pressure that I sometimes had, but if Kathleen had been actually driven to meet me, that was something more than pressure.

When I was interested in hypnotism, I had seen experiments in post-hypnotic suggestion, when under hypnosis a person was told that in, say, five minutes after being brought round he would do some specified thing, sometimes something quite ridiculous. At the end of five minutes he would do it, without being aware of what he had been told to do.

The puzzling thing is that I don't think anyone knows how these hypnotic suggestions work. If Satan knows how to reach the suggestive centre, and implants his own suggestions there, such as "Go to the lake at once," we could easily become puppets on a string. I had not reached any conclusion about the possibility of this by the time I left the main track and took the footpath to the lake.

I looked about for Kathleen, and at first couldn't see her. Maybe she had resisted the suggestion, and I was relieved. Then I saw her in a grey suit, sitting beside a flowering bush, and staring across the water which was flickering in the sunlight. I didn't know whether Satan had told her that she would be meeting me, but I began to walk noisily as I came near her, so as not to take her by surprise.

She turned and saw me. "Oh hello!" she said. "I hope it won't be like that time in the wood."

I sat down by her side. "No," I answered, "no mediumship this time." I didn't add, "And no kiss." I had no intention of making this an engagement party.

"He — you know who I mean — prompted me to come here. Why?"

"Yes, he told me to come here and meet you. He seemed to think it rather strange that since you know so much, we had never met to talk things over."

She picked up a small stone, threw it into the lake, dusted the earth from her hands, and looked at me. "Do you love ..." she hesitated for a moment, and then added, "him?"

Her question staggered me. It was something I had never even considered. I paused before answering. "... I serve him and obey him."

"I know that. But do you love him?"

"That's a difficult thing to answer."

"You ought to know."

I turned the question back on Kathleen. "You know we are all his servants here. Do *you* love him?"

"No," she said abruptly. "I fear him. If you were honest, you'd say the same."

"I can't discuss it now," I said, and changed the subject by asking, "Is there anything going on in the village that I ought to know?"

I think she wanted to follow up her question. She frowned, and answered almost at once, "Things aren't working out as they should. They're turning sour on us. There's an atmosphere of selfishness creeping in, and laziness too. Satan gives them all they want, and it isn't doing them any good. They want it — and they get it."

"Wait a bit," I interrupted. "Satan isn't giving them everything, and he does encourage do-it-yourself efforts".

"Not very often I'm afraid. And another thing. There are cliques springing up everywhere. Little groups meeting in each other's houses."

"What for?"

"Goodness knows. Some probably just for gossip, pulling other groups to pieces. I know some get together to drink. At least that's what it sounds like when they're going home. Some probably talk politics. At any rate, one or two have been getting Marxist books from the library, and other books on the political fringes. I think others have given themselves a sense of superiority by studying some of the literary classics. I've seen them grunting contemptuously when the person in front of them is taking out a light romance. I think you ought to know that a few of them are studying religion."

I said, "I hadn't realised there are religious books in the library. I'm surprised Satan allowed them."

"I checked them myself," she answered. "They're pretty general. Comparative religions and all that. Still, if they get talking, you never know what may happen."

"I'd no idea all this was going on."

"No. They obviously want to keep you in the dark. I wonder how much Satan knows."

I thought for a moment before commenting. "Probably everything, but I'm surprised he's not warned me."

"Does he really tell you everything?"

"If he wants me to take some action, yes. Otherwise I think he prefers people to settle their own affairs, so long as they're not disrupting the community."

"Don't you think you should call his attention to the religious group?"

"Maybe."

I felt prompted to pull a small notebook from my pocket, and my hand seized my pencil and wrote, *Let them talk away. Talking about religion never did anyone any harm.*

I showed the paper to Kathleen.

"So he uses automatic writing," she said. "And he's listening to everything we're saying."

Once more she picked up a stone and threw it in the water. I had a feeling she wanted to ask me another personal question. It came. "Tell me honestly. Do you feel you're a better person since you came here? I feel myself that I've somehow deteriorated. I can't put it into words, but I seem to have lost a lot of incentive."

"You're asking awkward questions," I said slowly.

"But what's the honest answer to this one? Tell me."

She pressed her hand on my knee, and looked into my face. I was annoyed, and pushed her hand away.

"I think we've said enough," I said, getting quickly to my feet. "Shall I see you home?"

"Thank you. I came by myself, and I can return by myself."

As I walked away, Kathleen was still sitting by the lake, throwing stones into the water.

I was even more angry on my way back than I had been when I came out. She was right, of course, about how I felt about myself.

CHAPTER 18

I had a bad night. I didn't get to sleep until after two, and was woken just before dawn by the sound of quiet feet coming to the front door, followed by the slight snap of the letterbox. By the time I'd made the effort to get up, there was no sign of anyone from the window, but there was a small folded note on the floor.

The early morning light was just bright enough for me to read it in the hall. *Please forgive me for yesterday. I must see you today. Same place, after the library closes at 5.00. Please come. K.*

I was disturbed. What had kept me awake in the night was Kathleen's voice repeating again and again in my brain, "Do you love him?" and "Do you feel you're a better person since you came here?" What was she going to ask next?

I decided to take a walk after breakfast. I went up past Kathleen's house, although I knew she would be at the library. As I was passing, I was surprised to see smoke coming from the chimney of the house next door. There was nothing surprising about a log fire, but this was the house where the Stuckeys had lived, and it was supposed to be empty now. As agent, I ought to know who was there.

I went up the path and knocked on the door. There was no reply, but I thought I heard a laugh. I knocked again, and after a further delay the door opened a little way, and I was confronted by Tom, the son of Bill and Betty Broadwood (he was the plumber), and behind him Pat the daughter of the printer Joe Penny and his wife Margaret. Tom glared at me, while Pat shrank back.

"I wondered who was living here now," I began.

"So now you know," he retorted. "Tom and Pat."

"You're living together, then?"

"Of course."

"May I come in and talk to you both?"

"No. There's nothing to talk about. We love each other, and we're living together. That's all there is to it, and it's no business of yours."

"I think it *is* my business. I've been put in charge of this village, and I've to see that things go smoothly. And you're not going to upset things."

"Okay, who put you in charge? *We* certainly didn't. You've told us about the crazy scientist who brought us here. We've never seen him. Is there really such a person, or are you responsible for everything?"

We were at an impasse.

Tom Broadwood went on, "Well, who made you the boss of the place? Why should we listen to you?"

He slammed the door, and left me standing there. There was nothing to do but leave. I had no idea what I ought to do. Fortunately, I had made no threats of any specific action that I might take. I had spoken of their living together as a disturbance to the community, and I felt I was right.

I suppose it was a hangover from my Christian days, but I couldn't see that living together in intimacy while unmarried was good policy in society. After all, almost every nation and tribe had found it expedient to have some form of marriage.

I went straight home, only to find four people waiting for me by my front door: the parents of the young people I had just seen.

Betty Broadwood ran out to meet me at the gate. "Mr Longstone, you must stop it at once," she shrieked.

Margaret Penny was quieter. "You must find them and bring them back."

"I've found them," I said. "But you must be the ones to get them back."

"Where are they then?" It was Betty Broadwood again.

"Come inside and I'll tell you."

We went in, in spite of Betty Broadwood demanding to go to them instantly.

I told them that I had found the two, and that they had spent the night together. I had spoken strongly to them, but they had insisted that they were definitely planning to live together.

"But they're not married!" wailed Mrs Broadwood.

Her husband Bill joined in. "What arrangements have you got for weddings? You don't have a church here."

"No. That's because none of us are Christians."

"We'd always hoped that our son would have a church

wedding, like we had."

"We can arrange a marriage without a church."

"You mean, like a registry office?" put in Margaret Penny.

"Yes, more or less. Do you want them to marry?"

There was dead silence. Then Joe Penny said hesitatingly, "I'm not sure that we do."

The others nodded. I saw a temporary way out.

"We'll arrange a marriage when you're all agreed. Meanwhile it's up to you to do what has to be done. It's hardly my job, and I could tell this morning that they won't listen to me. You'd better go and see them. They're in the Stuckeys' old house."

The two sets of parents hardly paused to say goodbye. I watched them hurry up the road. I sat down before I was aware of Satan in the armchair opposite. I felt he had come in the nick of time to solve my problem.

He began to speak before I could say anything. "You want my approval, don't you! Well, I *don't* approve."

I was surprised. "You mean, you're happy for those two to live together."

"Certainly. It won't disrupt the community. We have to encourage the young people, and if they want to live together and be free to separate if things go wrong, then let them do it."

"Excuse me," I said, "but what about their parents? They're disrupted enough."

"On the contrary. This is a Romeo and Juliet situation. The two families weren't on speaking terms until this happened, and now they're close — for a time. Anyway, you'd better stand back and let things take their course. It isn't like wife swapping. We couldn't have that. I'd have to take one of the couples away."

"Tell me, what line do you take on earth about this?"

"If you'd still been teaching theology, you'd have been talking about 'situation ethics'. They've at last discovered what I've been practising since the beginning. Seeing which way the cat jumps, and jumping with it. You want to know what I do? I prompt a clergyman, the higher up the better, to denounce couples who are living together without being married, and then prompt the media to denounce the church for its narrow-mindedness. In another situation I would call the media's attention to some sex scandal, and when the Sunday papers had exposed it with cries of horror, I would find some well-known churchman to soft soap the people in the name of charity. Anything will do to blacken the Christian church."

I thought of what Kathleen had said.

"You mentioned charity," I said. "Charity in the Bible is love. Have you any time for love?"

"Ah, you're thinking of your conversation yesterday with Kathleen Ryecroft. That woman put you on the spot when she asked you whether you loved me. At least you were honest. You don't love me, and I don't love you, and I don't love any of my helpers. The word is meaningless."

I broke in. "But you recognise that those two young people in the Stuckeys' old house love each other."

"Oh yes, I recognise sex attraction in the animal world. I hear it all the time in the world of pop. Spell it L-U-V if you want to."

"I'm a bachelor myself, but I recognise that good married L-O-V-E is something beyond L-U-V, which is where the pop songs stop. And I know there's something more, not only married love."

"My dear man, you've got a hangover from Christianity. It's one of those crazy ideas that drives people to sacrifice and martyrdom, and even to devotion to their so-called God. You don't imagine I've put you in charge here to *love* these people. You're fortunate that you can be boss and control them. They'd all like to be in your place. That's what life is all about."

It was an illuminating comment on human nature, and presumably on diabolic nature too. I didn't reply.

Satan changed the subject. "Now, I have something to tell you. You won't be in touch with me for a bit, unless there's a real emergency. I have to concentrate my efforts on fresh trouble in one part of the earth."

I felt for a moment like a soldier, on the death of his officer, suddenly finding himself in command. A sort of panic.

"Don't worry! You won't be on your own. You'll have my deputy, the spirit I've appointed as Prince of Priam."

My teaching days came back to me. "Daniel," I said to myself.

"Yes, Daniel was clever enough to realise I had my princes controlling the nations that tried to destroy his people. I still have."

"You've certainly got things organised, Satan. Was Saint Paul right when he spoke of fighting against principalities and powers and world rulers?"

"Of course. It's what I said just now. Give as many as possible a position of power, and you keep them happy. Even the lesser spirits like to pick up a sense of power by possessing or influencing anyone they can."

"So," I said, "I can still get any help I need from this Prince of Priam."

"That is so. He will be on our hot line. I'll be back as soon as I've settled the trouble in the Middle East. Oh, and by the way, Kathleen Ryecroft will be waiting for you by the lake a little after six this evening, after the library closes."

He was gone.

I must have fallen asleep with the exhaustion that always followed the psychic drain on my energy that enabled Satan to materialise. Conversation on the telepathic hot line didn't have the same effect. I decided to take an afternoon nap.

It was nearly four-thirty when I woke up. There was time for a cup of tea and a few biscuits before I had to go to meet Kathleen. I had to admit to being uneasy, especially after the recent conversation with Satan on L-U-V, and the earlier suggestion that I should marry her. I didn't know what might be in her mind, and I was definitely not going to let her sweep me off my feet.

I was at the lake in plenty of time, and sat down on the bank to wait. The early evening sun sparkled on the water. A flotilla of brown and blue ducks paddled by, and an occasional fish jumped with a scatter of water drops. I could see insects like mayflies swirling round and round above the water, and a blue and gold dragonfly settled on some grasses by the shore. It was a perfect evening. In fact, every evening was perfect on Priam, where the climate was balanced with rain and sunshine; the rain generally falling late at night.

With so much to enjoy, my thoughts had switched from the coming meeting, and I didn't hear Kathleen as she approached quietly through the grass. She was there beside me, looking down on me. She had dressed in grey, as before, and was smiling. I scrambled to my feet and motioned to her to sit down with me.

"I'm glad you could come, John," she said.

"It's a beautiful place," I replied.

She turned her head and looked at me. Her face was red. "If you're going to be cool with me, I'll go."

"I'm sorry, Kathleen. You have something you want to say?"

"I'm sorry if I upset you yesterday." She put her hand on my arm, and went on, "I need your help."

I had to come off my high horse. "I'm sorry again. What is it?"

"I must get away from this place."

"Now look," I said, "you realise they're listening in to everything we're saying."

"I know. But I must speak to you."

"What's getting you down?"

"It's the whole atmosphere. It's crushing me. I feel we're being watched all the time. I can hardly breathe. When I was young I had this really old motto on my bedroom wall, THOU, GOD, SEEST ME. I think it had been my grandmother's. I never knew whether it was a threat or a promise, but if there had been a god I never felt him with me. I'm only surprised, since you're psychic, that you haven't felt the same. Haven't you felt trapped and watched?"

I pondered. Had I felt it? I had been aware of a background, but I had treated it as part of the whole plan for my leadership. I could see what she was feeling, but I dared not face what I was feeling myself. I must keep to my duty.

"You know it's not possible to get away. We had all that out before Christmas."

"But, John, we're psychic. Surely that makes a difference. I've tried by myself, and I can experience astral projection, but I can't travel away from Priam."

"Then what do you want me to do?"

"Couldn't you lend me your psychic force to combine with mine?"

"It wouldn't work. We couldn't project your body through the galaxies to earth."

"I thought we might project my astral body to earth, and then somehow I'd anchor myself and attract my physical body to join me there, instead of my astral body being drawn back to the physical as always happens."

I shook my head. "No, I'm sure that wouldn't work. Don't you think you ought to stay here and face it out for the sake of others? After all, now that you know so much about what goes on behind the scenes, you can help me to keep things running sweetly."

Kathleen stared down into the water before answering. "It's funny, John. I believe at one time I would have thought just that. But now, no, I'm thinking more of myself than of others. Why should I sacrifice myself for them?"

"You know you'll have to stay. I daren't help you even if I could. I'm watched all the time."

"So you wouldn't sacrifice yourself for me, any more than I would for the others. If I don't get away, I'll go off my head."

"Why not ask the doctor for some tranquilisers?"

Kathleen laughed derisively. "John Longstone, I expected something better from you. I came asking for bread and you offered me tranquilisers. There's no point in going on."

She scrambled to her feet and I got up with her. She hesitated for a moment, and then said, "I suppose I'd better say everything I came to say. If my first idea was no good — and it evidently isn't — I was going to ask you about angels."

"What about them?"

"Well, we know now that there are goodness knows how many spirits under Satan. Could there be spirits on the other side, like Michael and others?"

"Certainly the Book of Revelation says that Michael and his angels fought against the devil and his angels, but Revelation is a strange book."

"A lot of people believe in guardian angels. Suppose they are just as real as Satan's angels. Couldn't I ask them for help?"

I felt uneasy. If there was anything in the idea, it seemed like going over to the enemy. I could only tell her that I didn't know.

"Then I'll try," she said, and moved quickly away.

I stood and watched until she had disappeared among the trees.

Two days later I went to the library and fidgeted among the books until two other borrowers had gone. Then I spoke to Kathleen at the desk. She looked drawn and tired.

"It's hopeless," she said. "I've relaxed, and appealed three times to an angel to help me, but all I got was a voice surging up inside me, saying, 'No angels here. No angels here.' And I've felt worse ever since. Whatever can I do?"

There were tears in her eyes as she reached across the counter and gripped my arms. "John, if only you felt it too! Then we could plan something together."

I slipped my arms from her grasp, and caught hold of her hands. They felt icily cold. "I'll stand by you, Kathleen," I said. "I want you to be free to tell me anything any time. We'll sort things out together somehow. But you must face it, you can't escape. And I have my loyalties here."

"Thank you," she said, and took her hands away. For a moment I felt that, if the counter had not been between us, she would have kissed me, as she did in the wood.

The door of the library opened and I moved away. Kathleen dived below the level of the counter, and when she stood up again she was perfectly composed.

CHAPTER 19

The days that followed were far from happy, but this had nothing to do with Satan's absence. His deputy the Prince of Priam carried on admirably. He opened up the hot line each day, and kept me informed of anything I needed to know, and was always ready with advice.

There was, however, one event that he didn't tell me about until afterwards. This was the calling of a meeting of the council. All the other five members were somehow notified, but I was left out. The Prince told me afterwards that it was better for me not to be involved, since Margaret Penny was raising the matter of her daughter Pat and Tom Broadwood living together. They had refused to listen to their parents, who wanted to separate them. My belief is that the Pennys didn't feel that the Broadwood boy was good enough for their daughter.

Satan's deputy gave me an outline of what was said at the meeting. Margaret Penny had abused me for not taking a stronger line, as she thought I could have done in my position. Bill Broadwood backed her. I imagine he had failed to understand, as I had, that his son was not regarded as good enough, but his wife had probably not let him forget the family scandal. Dave Sugden, the storekeeper, gave them half-hearted support, but Jim Token the farmer, and to my surprise the doctor, saw no reason to interfere.

Dr Faber, who in my absence was in the chair, closed the discussion by asking whether others had gathered that there was a growing opposition to my leadership. He had heard grumbles from his patients. What exactly was my position? I had kept referring to some superior, mysterious scientist, but no one had ever seen him. Did he, in fact, exist? If not, why shouldn't someone else be democratically elected to take on the leadership?

The others agreed that something should be done, provided it could be done without undue risk. After all, I seemed to have some secret power. Sugden suggested that they should call my bluff and make a unanimous demand to speak to this mysterious boss. If nothing happened, they would know I was romancing and sheltering behind an imaginary figure. If he appeared, as he surely could — since he had projected them all here — they could talk to him frankly about anything they had on their minds, and hopefully get straight answers. They agreed that the doctor should see me about this.

When the Prince of Priam told me what had been decided, I was worried that I couldn't consult Satan personally. I knew I couldn't give the doctor an immediate answer off my own bat. However, the Prince assured me he would keep Dr Faber from seeing me.

"How can you do that?" I asked.

"It's not difficult. I'll confuse his mind, so that every time he sets out to see you, he'll forget what he was intending to do."

"But suppose he meets me in the road."

"He'll forget what he wanted to say."

And this is what happened.

Meanwhile trouble blew up over money tokens. Everyone was entitled to draw tokens to the value of 600 points a month. This may not sound much, but the prices in the shop were fixed very low, and for example tins of food were no more than one or two points, except for luxury foods. It was possible to earn more by working on the farm or helping elsewhere. There was a standard wage of four points an hour. The employer didn't pay in tokens, but gave a note of the hours worked to be cashed at the bank. The employer himself was trusted to keep a note of the hours that he himself worked, less payment that he received for his services, such as, in the farmer's case, the sale of milk and vegetables.

By this time there was a noticeable difference between richer and poorer. Those who employed others, and those who worked for them, had many more tokens than housewives who couldn't take a job, or people who couldn't or wouldn't work. Those with more tokens apparently didn't trouble to save, but went in for expensive luxuries.

The result was that some were flashing their flamboyant life style, so that others, although they had sufficient, were being given a sense of inferiority. A deputation of wives came to see me. They asked for a bigger monthly ration. In return, I asked how many were actually in debt.

No one admitted to this, but one woman spoke up. "It's not fair, you see. Look at all the money some of them have. They're buying all sorts of things we can't afford."

I happened to look out of the window, and noticed a teenager whom I knew had been in regular work at the farm, and who must consequently have drawn a lot of tokens. I tapped on the window and beckoned him in. He looked round at the deputation in surprise.

"We're discussing having more tokens," I said.

"Suits me," he answered with a grin.

"I know you're working, but we think we should give more tokens for those people who aren't."

"If it's more for them, it's more for me, isn't it?"

"Why, you're not short."

"Maybe not short. But I can always do with more, can't I?"

"So can these people."

"Okay. If you raise their cash, you'll have to raise mine too. Don't forget that! Tata!" He went out, and slammed the door.

"Selfish pig," shouted one woman. The rest murmured agreement.

I didn't know what to say, but I promised that I would raise the matter with the Master who was ultimately responsible for our being here. They went away reluctantly.

I was not prepared for another deputation late in the afternoon. These were the "rich". The teenager had evidently told them about his morning experience.

Jim Token, the farmer, seemed to be the representative. He was a member of the council that had recently criticised me.

He began, "We understand you're considering raising the monthly tokens. That'll include ours, won't it?"

"Nothing's decided yet. But obviously, if the amount is raised, yours will be too."

"Then what about our work money. Will that be raised?"

"I don't see why it should be. The proposal is to help those who aren't able to earn extra."

"That wouldn't be fair. It'd upset the differential between us."

"Look," I said, "you've been able to afford all sorts of extras that these others don't have. Have you ever thought of buying one or two of these extras, like some special food or fancy clothes, for those who can't afford them?"

"Why should we? We've worked hard for these things for ourselves. Why should we give them away?"

"I'm sorry you take that line," I said. "I can only say that the two things will be considered together when I contact our higher authority."

"In other words, you're passing the buck. But I tell you what. If we don't get what we want, you'll have a strike on your hands. So far as I'm concerned, I'll pour the milk down the drain. And I know the workers at the power station will pull the switches, and there's no one else who can look after the turbines."

"We'll deal with that when the matter's decided, but I must say I don't like your attitude."

"Nor I yours."

"Then," I said with some heat, "there's nothing more to

discuss."

I showed them to the door.

Money came up again when a young widow with two young children was taken ill. She was Mrs Agnes Brown, who had a house at the end of the village. I had accepted her because Satan had told me to choose a mixed group to make up the community. She had some health problems, for which Dr Faber prescribed complete rest in bed for a few days.

It was the doctor who came to see me about her. I was amused when he began, "I know there was something I wanted to ask you, but for the moment I've forgotten it. But there is one thing. Mrs Brown isn't at all well. I needn't go into technicalities, but she'll be all right if she can rest in bed and be relieved of the children for a few days. She doesn't need intensive nursing."

"That needn't be much of a problem," I said. "I'm sure her neighbours will keep an eye on her, and one of them will take the children."

"Yes, that's what I thought. I'm sure that back home any of the neighbours would have done it. But something's happened to the people here. They won't move a finger unless they're paid for it."

"I'm sorry about that."

"I suggested that they might do it for love, but one of them told me that love wasn't cash. And I know they're not badly off."

"Do you think they should be paid?"

"If you think payment is the only solution, then do it, John. But the rule, as you know, is that the employer must give a paper to say how many hours have been worked. Agnes Brown is hardly an employer. Looking after her children will be an informal arrangement. I suppose it would be my responsibility to employ someone to keep an eye on her. But will I be the employer if the children join up with a neighbour's family? How many hours could they claim for? Twenty-four?"

I would like to have had time to consult the Prince of Priam, but the matter was urgent.

I nodded. "We'd better give way now, though goodness knows whether we're setting a precedent. I should think a twelve hour day would be fair for the reckoning, but of course deduct for school hours."

"I'll suggest that, and I don't imagine it'll be difficult to get help now that money is involved. Of course, it's a matter of principle. Otherwise there doesn't seem to be any shortage of tokens."

He hesitated a moment, and then went on, "I gather you're under some pressure to increase the payment for all work. Is it likely to go through?"

"Not if I can help it, but I may be overruled."

"In that case, you won't mind if I make an adjustment for myself and my wife. I've been charging for my surgery hours, morning and early evening, and for any calls I've made. But you'll appreciate the fact that, even if I'm not called out, I'm on duty all the time. I'd thought of twenty-four hours, but I'd be happy to settle for twelve. Also, Sarah pointed out that although she's my wife, she's been acting as my unofficial secretary, and has to be ready to deal with visitors at any time. So shall we say twelve hours for her?"

He bent down to pick up his bag. There was nothing I could say but Yes. I began to wonder what my own duties were? Twelve hours perhaps? It was up to the self-employed to give an honest answer. In fact, I had not drawn anything beyond my basic 600 tokens. But I was the agent, and it was hardly right that the agent should not draw what lesser men were drawing. Twelve hours pay was about right for the responsibilities I carried.

An hour later I looked out of the window, and involuntarily cried out, "Oh no! Not another deputation."

Two women bustled up to the door. I let them in, and one of them came straight to the point.

"Did you tell the doc to get Mrs Higgins and Mrs Davis to look after Agnes Brown and her kids?"

"I knew he was asking someone, but I didn't know who. What's the trouble?"

"We'd have done it if he'd given us the chance."

"You mean he didn't ask you?"

"Well, yes, he asked us this morning, but he didn't say we'd be paid."

"So you said No."

"Well, yes," said her companion. "But he's paying those others. He ought to have given us another chance."

"I don't see it," I said. "He probably thought you meant it when you refused."

"So we did. But then we weren't being paid."

"I'm sorry. The doctor's in charge of the case, and I can't interfere."

"We thought you were the boss. It's not good enough.

We all know why the doc chose those two. They're educated, like he is. They belong to the group that reads literature and that sort of stuff. We don't."

They got up, and pushed out of the door before I could show them out.

CHAPTER 20

This was not the end of the Agnes Brown affair. Three days later Dr Faber came again. Mrs Brown was going downhill and believed she was dying. She was in a state of acute depression and distress.

"I don't believe she's critical, but although she's still young, she's terrified of dying," the doctor explained. "If she goes on like this she may very well worry herself into the grave. Can you go and see her?"

"Have you been able to help her at all?"

He gave a half smile. "I talked to her about survival along the lines that I talked to you before Bill Stuckey's funeral."

"That was no good?" I asked.

"She said it was all talk, and she wanted something to cling on to."

"I can't see I could say any more than you did. Probably not as much."

"But at least you're an authority figure, the nearest she can get to a priest."

That made me jump. "A poor sort of priest, when I don't believe in God. But I suppose I ought to go, though heaven knows what I'm to say."

The doctor smiled. "Heaven knows? You're almost a priest already!"

I must admit I was too much of a coward to go alone. I thought of Kathleen Ryecroft as a possible helper. Perhaps as two psychically gifted partners we might be able to sense something that would help. I called at the library and explained the situation, and we arranged to go together at six o'clock.

Kathleen was waiting outside the house when I arrived. We agreed that she would go in first, and ask Mrs Brown whether she could do anything to help. I would come in after waiting two or three minutes.

When I went in, Kathleen was talking to Mrs Higgins whom the doctor had engaged to take care of the children for the time being.

Kathleen looked at me and said, "Oh, Mr Longstone, I was just telling Mrs Higgins that I'd take over, while she sees to her husband's supper."

Agnes Brown called from the bed, "You'll stay too, Mr Longstone, won't you?"

"Of course I will. Mrs Higgins will be back later."

Mrs Higgins looked round the room to check everything before leaving. She pointed to a bottle of medicine and a glass on the chest of drawers. "She won't be due for a dose till I get back."

"All right, Mrs Higgins, I'll stay on until you come."

After Mrs Higgins left, Agnes Brown began to turn

restlessly in bed, but every so often she stared hard at each of us. We sat silently by her side, until she spoke. I heard desperation in her young voice.

"I'm dying, you know."

Kathleen said, "I believe you'll get better."

And I added, "The doctor told me so."

"They always say that to try to cheer you up. But I know what I know."

"Are you worried about your children?" I asked.

"Yes, I am. But I'm sure they'll be looked after. People are kind. But everything's so dark. I'm going out into the dark. Can't you give me any hope?"

"There's always hope," I said.

"Not when you're dying. No one's ever come back from the dead to tell us."

"But we can still hope," Kathleen insisted.

Agnes Brown stayed silent for a minute, and then said in a tense voice, "I've not been all I should. I've been remembering things I wish I'd never done. What's going to happen to me?"

I thought of what the doctor had called me. "A sort of priest." A priest hears confessions, doesn't he?

Agnes Brown was moaning, "I want to be forgiven. It's all so dark. Tell me I'm forgiven. Can't you do something for me, Mr Longstone? I'm dying, and it's all so dark."

Kathleen caught my arm. "Do something, John. You must, before it's too late. Can't you sense the darkness?"

And certainly I could. A heavy cloud filled the room. I could smell evil, and a barrier of even deeper darkness came between me and the bed.

"You must, John, you must."

Kathleen's voice came to me from a distance. My mouth felt as though a hand was pressed over it to stop me from speaking. I knew the powers of darkness were against me.

Agnes Brown called again, "John," and her voice seeming to come from a distance was more desperate than ever. This time she called me by my Christian name. My *Christian* name. And I had once been a priest.

I fought my way to the bedside and laid my hands on the young widow's head. With all my might I forced the words through the barrier. "Agnes Brown, your sins are forgiven."

The darkness vanished. The pressure had gone. Kathleen was crying. And Agnes Brown's face was happy. She sat up in bed, and stretched out her arms towards someone whom we couldn't see.

"Oh miss," she called, and her voice sounded like the voice of a young child, "it's just like you told us in the Sunday school. I'm coming now."

Her voice returned to its normal tones. "Thank you, thank you!" she said, seizing my hand. "I'm happy now."

And she began to sing, once more in the voice of a child, "Safe in the arms of Jesus."

She had hardly sung the first line when she fell back on the pillow. I didn't need to touch her to know that she was dead.

Kathleen and I looked at each other. On occasions like this one tends to break the tension by some irrelevant remark. It may not have been entirely irrelevant, but Kathleen said, "I've not thought of it before, but John *is* your Christian name. Your *Christian* name."

"I prefer to think of it as my first name." I was anxious to change the subject, because she had echoed the exact words that had occurred to me a minute earlier. "What are we to do now?"

"Obviously we must fetch the doctor, but I'm sure she's dead."

We stared down at Agnes Brown. Kathleen put her head down, and tried to hear her heart. When she stood up, she said, "I can't hear anything. I'm sure she's dead. But if you like, I'll stay here while you go for Dr Faber."

I nodded, and went out. Fortunately, there was no one in the road to ask questions. When I told the doctor, he was frankly surprised.

"I hadn't expected her to go, certainly not so soon. Could you say anything to help her?"

"I did my best," I said. "Kathleen Ryecroft was there too, and she helped."

"Ah well, I'll go along in case there's anything I can do. You'd better come with me." He picked up his bag.

Kathleen was sitting quietly in one of the chairs. Dr Faber made a quick examination, and drew the sheet over the face of the dead woman.

"We'll lock up the house for the time being. Longstone here will doubtless arrange the funeral. But would you, Miss Ryecroft, be able to break the news to the children? A woman could probably do it better than a man. And we must see whether Mrs Davis will keep on mothering them. Mrs Higgins will see to what needs to be done here if I ask her."

We went out together. The doctor locked up and took the key to Mrs Higgins. Kathleen went to Mrs Davis to see the children, and try to help them through the first shock. I asked her to come to my house afterwards.

It was getting dusk when she came. She was obviously under strain, and tired, and I had the kettle boiling for a pot of tea. She sank back in the armchair opposite to mine, and covered her face with her hands.

"You're tired, aren't you!" I said, rather obviously. "You've been through a lot. How are the children?"

"Better than I had expected. Do you know, it was almost as though they were half expecting something of the sort. Mrs Davis is going to keep them."

Kathleen seemed to be going over something in her mind as she sipped her tea. Presently she looked at me over the top of her cup. "What really happened just now?"

"It's obvious," I said. "Mrs Brown was hallucinated, and went back to her childhood. It can be done under hypnotism. You can suggest a person to be back at the age say, of six, and they will talk to some invisible person in the voice of a child, as they did at that age."

"Then you don't think she really saw her Sunday school teacher coming to welcome her as she was dying."

"Just hallucination," I said.

"I don't like to ask you, but were you just pretending when you told her that her sins were forgiven?"

It wasn't easy to answer. Was I pretending — or not? "Remember, I was once a priest, and I knew what comforted people. So I thought I would say the words."

"But were her sins forgiven? And what did she mean by

'safe in the arms of Jesus'?"

"It's an old hymn, and she evidently remembered it from Sunday school. And I've no idea about her sins."

"Then who did she think had forgiven them?"

"God, I suppose. I slipped up in choosing her. I hadn't realised that childhood religion can last so long, even when it's been dropped."

Kathleen put her cup down noisily on its saucer. Her face flushed. "Then I think you're a hypocrite."

"Wait a minute," I said. "Don't you remember it was you who told me to do something when she was worried about her sins. Weren't you the hypocrite? You weren't concerned about forgiveness, but you obviously wanted me to pretend her sins were forgiven."

She covered her face with her hands. "I'm sorry," she whispered. "It was all so real at the time, and yet you've explained it all away."

"If I hadn't explained it away, I'd be in hot water with Satan."

"So that's your reason. You wouldn't dare to think whether Mrs Brown knew something you don't know."

I stared at her in amazement. "That's dangerous talk on Priam, Kathleen. I'd advise you to dismiss it from your mind. If you're thinking of becoming a Christian, you'll be in danger. Don't forget that there's always one of Satan's servants listening. I'd hate anything to happen to you."

"Do you really mean that?" she said, searching my face.

"Of course I do. We're working together, and your advice can be useful to me.'

"Oh, is that all."

Suddenly I saw Kathleen in a new way. She was wanting me for herself, and as our eyes met I knew I wanted her. Satan had said that I could marry her, but I'd not taken his permission seriously. The prospect of marriage was something I'd quickly dismissed. But now, as I looked at Kathleen, marriage with her took on a new meaning.

We reached across, and our hands met.

"No, Kathleen," I said, "that isn't all. It's only the beginning."

I knew it was a strange sort of proposal, but we both understood. She came across to me, and I held her in my arms for a long time. We didn't say much, but my thoughts were travelling back over the times we had been together before, and I knew that even then there were the beginnings of an unrecognised love.

I remember we talked of future plans, and I remember we agreed to say nothing at present about our sudden engagement. It was only after Kathleen had left that I was struck by a frightening thought: was Kathleen on the way to becoming a Christian? Would this cause our first quarrel?

That night I dreamt, not of Kathleen, but of Agnes Brown.

CHAPTER 21

The next few days were trying. First, there was the funeral of Agnes Brown. I was not too happy with my address at Bill Stuckey's funeral, and I saw no point in speaking at this one. One or two asked me what I intended to do, and I told them there would be a simple burial without any address.

Then, when I saw Mrs Davis, who had taken on the children, she said that a funeral couldn't possibly take place without an address. She, as one of the literature group, would like to recite two verses that she remembered from one of Longfellow's poems. She was sure that these would be appreciated as a tribute to Agnes.

I asked Mrs Davis to let me hear the verses so that I could judge whether they were suitable. So she drew herself up, and said in a confident voice:

"There is no flock, however watched and tended,

But one dead lamb is there!

There is no fireside, howsoe'er defended,

But has one vacant chair!

The air is full of farewells of the dying,

And mournings for the dead;
The heart of Rachel, for her children crying,
Will not be comforted!"

"Is that all?" I asked, somewhat relieved at this solution to what could be a problem.

"That's all I remember."

"Then it will do very well. Thank you for the suggestion."

About an hour later, two women came to complain about the doctor's choice of Mrs Higgins and Mrs Davis.

"Is it true Mrs Davis wants to say something at the funeral?"

"Not exactly say something. She's going to recite a tribute to Agnes Brown."

"You mean she wants to show off. We told you she belongs to the fancy literature group."

"Then what do you suggest? Do either of you want to say something? You've very welcome to take part."

"We're no speakers. But it isn't fair you chose her. She's no better than anyone else."

I had some difficulty in getting rid of them, after explaining that no one else had come forward, and the words were very suitable.

So in due course the funeral took place outside the village, beside Bill Stuckey's grave. However, there had been a further upset about this, since Stuckey had a bad reputation, and one or two didn't want to see Agnes buried near him.

I felt exhausted after the funeral, and was settled in my armchair when Kathleen opened the door and came in. I greeted her, and she came over and kissed me before sitting down opposite. She came straight to the point.

"That poem. I recognised it. We had to learn it by heart at school, and it all came back to me."

"Well," I said, "I thought the two verses were very suitable."

"But if she'd recited the whole poem, you wouldn't have thought it was suitable."

"What does it say?"

She began to recite:

"She is not dead — the child of our affection —

But gone unto that school

Where she no longer needs our poor protection,

And Christ himself doth rule."

"I'm glad she didn't remember that verse," I said, biting my lip. "I was rather afraid when she mentioned Longfellow, because I knew that he was a Christian."

"I suppose Longfellow couldn't have been right in that verse, could he?" she said softly.

I felt angry. "Kathleen, we've only just come to know each other, and you're trying to spoil it all."

"Why me? Suppose Longfellow's right."

"Look here!" I answered her. "You've probably never thought out your position. I didn't throw over my Christianity easily. I weighed up all the arguments, and reached a firm decision. There *is* no God, and Jesus Christ was no more than a good man."

She murmured something under her breath.

"What's that you're saying?" I demanded.

"Just back at school again. I was remembering some

lines from Robert Browning's poem, *Bishop Blougram's Apology*. The bishop was an intellectualist like yourself, arguing over his doubts. Listen:

"The gain? How can we guard our unbelief,
Make it bear fruit to us? — the problem here.
Just when we are safest, there's a sunset-touch,
A fancy from a flower-bell, someone's death,
A chorus-ending from Euripides,
And that's enough for fifty hopes and fears
As old and new at once as Nature's self,
To rap and knock and enter in our soul."

I heard her through. Then I said, "It doesn't work like that when you've been into everything. You can be certain.'

She quoted again, "A fancy from a flower-bell, someone's death."

"I see. You've got that woman's death on your mind."

"Maybe I have. It moved me at the time, and it's haunted me since."

"Kathleen, emotion is not the way to discover truth."

"I was hoping it discovered true love for us, John."

"That's different. You can't go on talking like this. You know as well as I do that we're all here to demonstrate that a community can be happy and successful without being governed by ideas of God."

She looked so serious. "John, *are* we demonstrating it? We're no better than we were on earth. I think we're all getting worse. It's so gradual that we don't realise it. We're more and more living for ourselves. I see it in talking to people in the library. Everyone's wanting to be top dog, to have more and more. I'm all right Jack — that's it."

I was astonished at her outburst. But worse was to come.

"I don't think it's done you any good, John, since Satan took you up."

"Kathleen, I love you. But if we go on talking like this, we shall spoil everything. I'll be frank with you. If you're serious about Christianity, I can't marry you."

"Exactly," she said. "That's what I mean. You wouldn't marry me because then you'd lose your position. I'm all right Jack, and Kathleen's all wrong."

I controlled my anger, but I didn't kiss her as she left.

Next day I had a visit from the doctor.

"I don't know whether you are aware," he began, "that Jeremy Jenkins is holding healing meetings in his front room on Thursday evenings."

I told him this was news to me, and asked how long it had been going on. He told me that several times patients had told him that Jenkins had come in and laid his hands on them.

"Did they get better?" I asked.

"They all got better, but I was treating them too."

"So nothing miraculous?"

"Well, there have been three or four cases where a patient has recovered immediately after Jenkins' visit, when I would have expected him or her to take longer."

"And you say he's now taking healing sessions for anyone who cares to come on Thursdays."

"Yes, I don't suppose it matters, but I thought you ought to know."

"Many thanks. I think I'll have a word with him and find out just what's happening."

Secretly I was afraid that Jeremy Jenkins might be psychic, and become a third one in the secret of Priam. I knew Jenkins as a small, mild and insignificant man, whom I had judged to be an introvert type. I had known nothing of his healing powers, but since he had been on Priam he had caused something of a sensation by bringing in from the woods a yellow doglike animal that he called a doggo. It had black stripes, and he tamed it very quickly, and trained to do tricks. He actually called it Doggo as its name, and he used to give demonstrations on the green with this creature when the children came out of school.

He also was remarkably successful with his garden, and produced fine results, with vegetables at the back and flowers in the front. He had ordered seeds through the shop, but had also gathered some from the fields. On Priam, plants grew very quickly. I walked up and called on him. A handwritten notice in the window advertised the healing session on the coming Thursday, and private appointments if desired.

Jeremy Jenkins seemed surprised to see me, but welcomed me in. "Good morning, Mr Longstone. I take it you haven't come for healing."

"That's what I want to see you about."

His face tightened. "There's nothing wrong with offering healing. You can't stop me."

"I'm not trying to stop you. I'm interested in your gift. Would you say you were psychic?"

He brightened up at the opportunity of talking to someone who seemed to understand. "I know what you mean. I suppose healing is psychic, but I haven't any other psychic gifts, unless you count an ability to make friends with animals and birds. And I've got what they call green fingers for the garden."

"But no gifts of clairvoyance, or seeing the future?"

He shook his head, and I felt that the secret was still safe.

"Then, when did you discover your gift of healing?"

"When I was quite young, I felt prompted to put my hands on people who were suffering, and they told me they felt better, and some felt a warmth flowing into them from my hands."

"Then you never felt you were guided or inspired by spirits?"

"I don't believe in spirits. The power is in *me*."

"The doctor tells me you've been helping some of his patients here."

"Yes, but there are others the doctor doesn't know about. That's why I'm holding my own surgery."

"You never told me you were a healer when I interviewed you to come here."

"I didn't advertise it on earth. I only healed when I felt there was someone I could help. I healed two cases of cancer, but told them not to say anything about me. But up here — just look at me!"

He rose from his chair, and drew himself up to his full, small height. "Now look at me. They think I'm not much of a man."

He wasn't.

"Not much of a man," he went on. "No woman would look at me twice. But I can show them. I've got what they haven't got. I'm a healer. I'm the only one who's been able to tame a doggo. And my garden is the best in the village."

I was somewhat taken aback. "Certainly," I said, "you have great gifts."

"Gifts, you say? But they're *my* gifts, for me to use, and I've used them to put me on top."

There was little more that I could add, so I assured Jeremy Jenkins that I was most interested. His doggo got up from somewhere in the background, and watched me leave.

This desire to be top was brought home to me again that afternoon when I walked up to the level patch outside the village which was used as a football field. Soon after our arrival there was naturally a wish for football. Although I'm not a player, I encouraged it, and arranged for balls and posts to be teleported. It is true that Satan's servants made the mistake of sending up rugby balls, but the mistake was quickly put right, and games began.

They started simply as kickabouts, but very soon we found that the numbers who wanted to play came equally from both sides of the long village street. There were not enough to form two teams of eleven, but it was possible to pick two reasonably good teams of seven from each side of the street, with one or two extras if they were needed. Quite a number of the villagers turned out to support what was literally their side — their side of the street.

At first the matches were friendly affairs, played in good part, without even a referee. But by degrees a thirst for victory seemed to grow at all costs, and a ref had to try to control some nasty incidents.

This afternoon I could see that feelings were running high. I had been watching one player who looked rather better than the rest, when it dawned on me that he was on the wrong side. He belonged to the opposite side of the street. I spoke to a young man who was standing by me.

"We've bought him," he said. "We had a whip round, and paid him the tokens he wanted, more than the other side could manage. Good, isn't it!"

I felt sad as I turned away and went home. I hadn't expected that Priam would follow major football teams back home, who for decades had hired mercenaries to play the game in place of the local lads.

There were several injuries for the doctor to treat after the match. When the Prince of Priam opened the hot line, I asked what he could do about this thing that was spoiling the harmony of the community. He indicated that there was no solution short of direct interference, such as banning football altogether, or removing the ball.

"We can muddle the minds of the players, but that's a poor sort of solution. Unfortunately we can't change their hearts, which would give a permanent result."

When Kathleen looked in, I told her.

"Yes," she said, "a new heart. I've heard that some-where. But I've thought about what I said. Our love is too precious to spoil. I'll go along with what you believe."

This time I kissed her when she left. But you know how it is when someone capitulates, and you've won your argument. You suddenly feel more lenient, no longer needing to stand up for yourself. You can think of your opponent's points in a more relaxed way. Kathleen had surrendered her questioning beliefs to the love we felt for each other. But had she a right to do so?

After dark, I went out into the garden and looked up into the sky. There were more stars than I had ever seen on earth, and Priam's mini-moon was climbing the sky.

"Who made all these?"

My question, spoken aloud to no one but myself, startled me. I closed my mind to all the arguments I had once known, that creation implies God as creator. But was Satan the creator? I wouldn't dare to ask him.

CHAPTER 22

A few days later Satan's deputy, the Prince of Priam, told me that he was handing me back to his master. This information he communicated in the usual way by what I've described as the telepathic hot line. I thanked the deputy aloud for the help he had given, knowing he could somehow hear me. But I sensed some embarrassment.

"I don't want thanks. I can only do my duty."

"You say 'can' only do your duty. Don't you want to do what you're doing?"

"I don't choose what I want. I hold my power because my mind is one with my master."

"So there *is* something that you want for yourself. Power at the top? And you choose to keep in your place by obedience?"

"Obedience is the only way."

"Aren't all your master's servants obedient?"

"Some of them on earth go out on their own."

"How do you mean?"

"They find someone with a surplus of psychic energy,

and use this to become poltergeists. Or they fake messages through mediums. Or perhaps they look for humans who are experimenting with things like Ouija boards and table rapping, and when the group has generated enough psychic energy they sense it, and impersonate a real or fictitious character."

"But you wouldn't do that?"

"I am a higher power. I was given the position of Prince, to guide your community into obedience to my master, so that he can possess a kingdom of perfect harmony where human behaviour tallies with submission to his wishes."

"Thank you for talking so frankly," I said aloud, knowing he could hear. Then I couldn't resist adding, "I hope you haven't chosen to speak too much on your own initiative."

"All I have said has been for the good of the plan. John Longstone, you are *not* a Prince, but you are my master's human deputy here, and much that applies to me applies to you also. Do not step out of line with Kathleen. I bid you goodbye."

The line closed.

Early next morning, a hammering on the door woke me from a restless sleep. It was just after six o'clock, and the noise went on at intervals until I had put on my dressing gown and opened the door. Jeremy Jenkins, the healer, was jumping about on the doorstep, his face contorted with crying.

"What on earth has happened?" I asked.

I couldn't hear what he was trying to say, so I put out my hand and led him into the house. "Tell me what it is!" I demanded, as he sank down in the armchair.

He drew his hand across his face. "He's killed my Doggo, my lovely Doggo, and ruined my garden."

"Who are you talking about? Who's done it?"

"That Harry Haskins. He's had it in for me for weeks."

"Tell me. What's he done?"

With more tears, the story gradually came out. Harry Haskins lived two houses away. He too was a gardener, and the two were rivals. Lately, Jeremy Jenkins' garden was so much ahead of his rival's that neighbours were making comparisons. A week ago Harry Haskins had cut his leg badly, and although the doctor had treated it, his leg had swollen up.

"He knew I was a healer, and he came round to ask me to help him. The trouble is that I haven't the power to heal *everybody*. Generally, I can sense beforehand whether I can or not. I knew I couldn't heal Harry Haskin's leg, and I told him so. He got angry, and demanded that I should try. So in the end I laid my hands on him, but nothing happened, and he came back yesterday to tell me he was even worse. He accused me of refusing to heal him, out of spite."

"Well," I said, "he obviously felt you had something against him, but how do you know Harry did what you say he did?"

"I'll tell you. I woke up about three o'clock this morning, as Doggo was howling. I thought he needed to go out, so I went down to open the back door. Before I did so I looked out of the window, it was moonlight, and I could see Harry Haskins slashing about with a spade."

I interrupted. "One minute. Are you sure it was Harry?"

"I know him well enough. Besides, he was limping with his bad leg. I could see then why Doggo was making such a noise, and I didn't see why I shouldn't let him loose. So I opened the back door and he ran out. I heard a shout, and a thud, and then there was silence. I ran into the garden in time to see Harry Haskins struggling through the gate into the field. I could have caught him, but there was Doggo lying on the path. I bent down to him, but he was dead."

Once more Jeremy Jenkins was overcome with crying. At last he said, "And now this morning I discovered that my whole garden is ruined — everything chopped down or trampled down. What are you going to do about it, Mr Longstone?"

"I'm very sorry indeed. It's a terrible thing to happen. I'll certainly go and see Harry first thing this morning."

I put the kettle on, and we had a cup of tea before he left. I watched him walk slowly down the path, dragging his feet, his head bowed. I wasn't looking forward to an interview with Harry Haskins, but I went to his house immediately after breakfast.

His wife opened the door to me. "Harry guessed you'd come," was all she said, as she motioned me to come in.

"Here's Mr Longstone!" she called out, and Harry came in limping from the kitchen.

His first words were, "I suppose you've heard his story."

I nodded, and he went on, "But I don't suppose he's told you everything."

"He told me you did it, and he told me you didn't like him."

"Yes, I did it, and I *don't* like him. But there's more behind it than that."

"Tell him, Harry," said his wife, who had stayed in the room with us.

I listened without interrupting while Harry told me his side of the story. "You know we're both gardeners. Somehow his garden is always better than mine, and he rubs it in with the neighbours. He brings some of them round to the field at the back to look over the fence, first at his garden and then at mine. I know his crops are better. I think he must have some magic about him. He's a silly little man, and his garden is the one thing that gives him status, apart from that weird creature that he had as a pet."

He paused, and suggested to his wife that she should make a pot of tea. She went out, but left the door open.

"I cut my leg badly the other day, and it wouldn't heal. That man calls himself a healer. Maybe he is, and I've heard he's done some people good. But I've also heard of some funny goings-on in his front room when the curtains are drawn. He talks about laying on of hands, but I wouldn't let my wife have his hands laid on her if she was alone."

The kettle must have already been on the boil, for at this moment his wife came back with a tray. She stirred the pot, and poured out three cups.

"I think we can all do with a cup," she said, as she handed one to me and helped me to a generous spoonful of sugar.

Harry rattled his spoon round noisily in his cup, swallowed down a mouthful, and went on. "My leg was hurting, and I thought it might be worth letting byegones be byegones and seeing if that Jenkins fellow could do me any good. But would you believe it, he turned me down flat. Just said he couldn't do it. I don't mind telling you, I was angry. I told him I didn't think much of his claims if he wouldn't even try. So he put one hand on my leg, but I guess he switched his magic off first, because it didn't make the slightest difference. I felt mad that I'd humbled myself to come round to him and he'd simply gloated over me. And before I left he had the cheek to take me to the window, and suggest that I might like to see his garden."

Harry rattled the spoon in his cup again before taking another gulp of tea. I sipped mine.

"I couldn't sleep last night. My leg was hurting bad, and I thought it might help if I got up and walked round a bit. I looked out of my bedroom window which looks out over the gardens, and in the moonlight I saw the tops of plants in Jeremy Jenkins' garden, some sort of sweetcorn I think, and I just went mad. My wife takes sleeping pills and she was fast asleep. I went downstairs and out of the back door. I took a spade from the shed, and went along to his garden."

He had another gulp of tea.

"I began to lay about me with my spade, and then that blessed creature began to howl and throw himself against the kitchen door. I knew he couldn't get at me, so I went on hitting and trampling. Of course Jeremy Jenkins woke up, and suddenly the door opened and the creature came straight at me. I only thought of defending myself, and took a swing at it with my spade. I must have hit it on the side of the head as it sprang at me, and it dropped to the ground.

The only thing left was to escape before Jenkins caught me, and that's what I did."

The two stories posed a problem. I could imagine the insignificant little man boosting his image with his healing, and maybe feeding his vanity with women who came to him, and also his pride in the creature he had tamed. But now I had listened to the story of the strong man who believed he had been baited by the little man with his magic, and who thought his plea for healing had been deliberately spurned out of spite.

Quite honestly I didn't know what to do. Perhaps it was cowardly, but I felt I must throw the responsibility back on Satan. I might try the council, but I remembered that I was no longer *persona grata* with them. In any case, I would need Satan's advice.

CHAPTER 23

Kathleen looked in at lunchtime, and we had a couple of boiled eggs and toast together. My usual cooking wasn't elaborate. Naturally she had heard the news, since nothing else had been talked about in the library. She told me that opinions were divided over the two men. Some were upset that the doggo had been killed. It had been a favourite with the children. Others disliked Jenkins, and didn't mind him being taken down a peg.

Kathleen added her own comment. "I must say I'm not keen on Jeremy Jenkins myself. A woman often has an intuitive sense for these things that a man doesn't have. I wouldn't trust myself alone with him in his front room."

"Do you feel like that about all men?" I asked.

"Fishing for compliments, are you, Mr Longstone? Well, perhaps not *all* men."

I responded in kind. "Now who are you getting at, Miss Ryecroft, I wonder?"

She blew a kiss across the table.

I was surprised that Satan didn't open the line at the usual time. His observers had obviously told him what had happened, and I wondered whether he himself was puzzled over what action to take. When he communicated next day, I asked him what I should do.

"Nothing," he said. "If our community is to run smoothly, we must let the trouble die down. Once you start interfering, people will begin to take sides actively, and whichever side you take you'll get some of the blame. That won't be good for you as my deputy. It would have been better if it had never happened, but once it has, ignore it."

"Suppose both men appeal to the council?"

"They won't. They've both got things that they wouldn't like to be made public in court. Let them be."

I had anticipated Satan's answer, because, before he came through, a more serious tragedy happened. Soon after midnight I was woken by shouts of "*Fire!*"

I flung on some clothes and dashed out into the street. Not far off I could see flames leaping up from a house. As I came nearer, I saw it was the house occupied by Joe Penny the printer and his wife Margaret, the couple whose daughter Pat was living with Tom Broadwood in the Stuckeys' empty house.

As I ran, I could glimpse figures silhouetted against the flames. The house was well alight when I reached it, and neighbours clustered in the road well away from the heat. Two or three were running up with buckets of water, and I realised that Satan had slipped up over the provision of hydrants and hoses.

At that moment, a figure staggered out of the door and collapsed on the path. I could see a flame on the bottom of his pyjama jacket, and two of us dashed forward and tore it off his back. We dragged him to the gate in a state of semi-consciousness.

"Where's Margaret?" I shouted.

Someone in the crowd shouted back, "She's not come out."

A girl's voice called, "It's my mum. She's still in there."

The front door was still open after Joe had burst out, and we could see flames roaring up the stairs. It seemed impossible for anyone to get to the bedroom that way.

"Fetch a ladder, someone!" I called. "The window's our only hope."

"Right! I know where I can get one," a voice shouted.

But just then the girl's voice cried out again, "*No, Tom, no! Not you!* Please, someone, save my mum!"

Next moment a figure dashed past me, and young Tom Broadwood flung himself through the door. I could see a narrow strip by the wall that was still free from the flames which had crept up the banisters. Up this space and out of my sight Tom struggled. We waited for an eternity.

Then a face at the window, and another face beside the first. Tom had his prospective mother-in-law in his arms. He freed one arm to raise the window, and looked down on us below. I don't know what he could have done if the ladder had not arrived at this moment.

"Carry her down," Tom shouted, and the man with the ladder climbed clumsily up and somehow took hold of the unconscious woman, and came half sliding down with her. Tom followed. In the light of the flames I could see that his face was blackened, and he put his hand to his head as soon as he was on the ground.

Dr Jenkins had arrived, and examined Joe on the ground. Now he came over to Margaret his wife, and knelt down by her. He had a torch, which he placed on the grass, while he put his stethoscope to her chest. Then he shone the torch on her eyes.

Pat Penny had flung herself on Tom at the foot of the ladder, and it was a minute or two before she came to where the doctor was bending over her mother.

"Are they all right, doc?" she asked anxiously, as she looked first at her mother, and then across at her father.

"Your father will be all right when we've treated his burns. And yours too, young man," looking at Tom.

"Isn't my mum all right too?"

The doctor got up slowly, and put his hands on Pat's shoulder. "I'm sorry," he said. "I'm afraid there's nothing we can do. I knew she had a bad heart, and the shock's been too much for her."

Pat fell on her knees and kissed her mother's face again and again. Tears glistened in Tom's eyes. He put his arms round Pat and drew her to her feet. She looked down once more before burying her face on his shoulder, and moaning, "Why's she so cold when the fire's so hot?"

I admired Tom Broadwood, not only for his bravery but for the way he now took command. "Doctor, will you bring Dad to our house. He'll be living with us now, of course."

Pat looked up. "Yes, of course. He'll come to us."

"Thank you," the doctor said. "We'll see that he comes to you. But I'll need to see his burns first in my surgery — and yours too, Tom."

CHAPTER 24

It was a tragic end to the night, and I was aware of an atmosphere of gloom over the village next day. I looked in to see Tom and Pat, and Pat's father, and found both the invalids much better. Young Pat was bustling about caring for them, while her father Joe lay on a couch. He had obviously been shattered by the death of Margaret his wife. I think Pat was sustained by relief at having Tom safe, and by the thought of his bravery. I promised to make all the arrangements for the funeral.

On the way out, I met Tom Broadwood's parents coming to the house. Pat had shown me to the door, and Tom's mother ran forward and threw her arms round her. They had not been on speaking terms ever since the time when Tom and Pat had gone to live together. Tom's father had his arm round Pat's waist as they went into the house.

The wretched lines of a hymn flickered into my mind. *God moves in a mysterious way his wonders to perform.* "Does Satan?" I wondered aloud.

I hadn't long to wait for an answer, for that afternoon

Satan opened up the line again. Although the Prince of Priam had done all that I could expect, I somehow felt more reassured when dealing with Satan himself. Now I was able to question him about Jeremy Jenkins and Harry Haskins, and then about the fire.

"Why did you allow it?" I asked.

"How could I help it? I can't control all human folly. Joe and Margaret Penny pushed an armchair up against an electric fire without switching it off before they went to bed."

"Yes, but someone died, and Tom could easily have lost his life trying to rescue Margaret."

"The woman already had a bad heart, so I couldn't help her death. And Tom, I'm afraid, was a fool to risk his life."

"You don't really mean that."

"Of course I do. Why should he risk his life, especially for the woman who disliked him? If he'd done it for Pat, I might have understood a bit."

I must say I was astounded by this.

Satan went on, "You and I are setting up a viable community. This means that members must enjoy life for as long as possible. If, for example, you yourself had dashed into the flames and been killed, that would have been a big setback for me."

"Then you don't approve of sacrifice for others?"

"What's the point? All this idea of sacrifice owes a lot to the crazy fancies of Jesus. He wouldn't listen to me when I offered to give him all he wanted, and he went on to sacrifice himself for others, as he thought, on the cross. And what good did it do the others? A whole lot of them had to suffer too, and were martyred, with the same crazy notion of sacrifice."

I felt bound to intervene. "Christians would say it isn't just sacrifice in itself, but they are inspired by love."

"Love!" Satan snapped. "We've talked about that before. I don't understand love, though I admit that there's something called love that drives people to marry. I admit it, but can't understand it, because it's something physical, and I don't have a body."

"Not even when you materialise, as you have done when you've let me see and talk to you?"

"Maybe I could get somewhere near it. But I learnt my lesson long ago in the time of Noah. A whole lot of spirits liked the look of human girls, and materialised enough to have sexual intercourse with them, a thing that their natures didn't allow them to do amongst themselves as spirit beings. There was a lot of psychic energy being let loose at that time, even among the girls themselves, so there was plenty that the spirits could use for materialisation."

"You say you learnt a lesson from them."

"Yes. They put themselves into a position where they were neither human nor pure spirit, and they vanished into a kind of limbo. So I was unable to use them among my servants."

I couldn't resist showing off my knowledge of the book of Genesis and Peter's second New Testament letter. "I remember Peter says that those spirits were imprisoned in Tartarus."

I wondered how Satan would take this quoting of the

Bible, but I need not have worried. He said, "I can quote Scripture too. Jude in his letter says they are kept in chains in the darkness."

"I've read these things in the Bible, but imagined they were just superstition."

"Take it from me, they're true. The Bible contains plenty of facts. The trouble is that the writers, who recorded them, felt bound to overlay them with theories about a so-called God. They were wrong. You need to take the facts, yes, but leave God out. Some of your own theologians have done that. Isn't that why you yourself threw over what you were pleased to call The Faith?"

"Yes," I said. "I found God was dead, so his place in the Bible was all imagination."

Before I had time to argue further and give the matter some thought, Satan quickly changed the subject.

"You'll find the doctor is coming to see you. You remember that the council commissioned him to ask you to bring me here for everyone to interview. While I was away, my deputy muddled the doctor's mind so that he kept forgetting what he had to do, but now I'm ready."

"You mean, I can tell Dr Faber you'll come."

"Yes, but I'm not going to be at anyone's beck and call. I'll appear when I wish, and not before. I know a lot of people here think I don't really exist, and won't believe in me until they see me. So tell them I'll appear, but they won't know until just beforehand. Then I shall need psychic power from you and Kathleen to help a big materialisation."

I heard no more. The line was dead.

* * *

Dr Faber chose to speak at the funeral. He expressed a hope of survival after death, but concentrated on praising Tom Broadwood's bravery and expressing our sympathy with Joe Penny and his daughter Pat for their loss. It was a relief to me not to have to speak. Afterwards, Tom Broadwood and Pat Penny wanted to discuss marriage.

Sure enough, the doctor looked in to see me next morning. He sat in "Satan's" armchair.

"I've had a lot on my mind lately," he began, "and I've kept forgetting a request I was asked to put to you."

"Go on," I said.

"Well, I can remember it now. Quite a lot of us are anxious to meet your master. There are a few things we want to ask him. In fact, I'm afraid there are two or three who don't believe he really exists, and that you're using this imaginary person to back up your own ideas, and save yourself from blame if things go wrong."

"Very flattering, I'm sure," I said with a smile. "So I've all these terrific powers? I only wish I had!"

"If it's not you, we want to see this superman of yours. He appears to be a miracle worker, so surely he can do for himself what he did for us, and bring himself here."

"All right. As a matter of fact he has already promised to come, and you will all see him."

Peter Faber leaned forward in his chair. "That's good news. That's what we want to hear. When will it be?"

"He doesn't know, but he's promised to come when he can."

"Not very satisfactory, but I suppose we'll have to be

content with that. These scientists are often quite unpredictable. Well, I'll tell the others what you've told me."

He got up to go. I showed him to the door.

I can't pretend that I enjoyed the days that followed. Satan was silent when I tried to open up the line. I sensed that the whole village was getting restless. I found a slogan daubed on my gate. WHAT ABOUT HIS PROMISE TO COME? I washed it off, but I was worried.

I suppose a month had gone by when Kathleen came to me after dark one evening.

I had seen her at odd times lately, and I don't think anyone suspected there was anything between us. She looked serious as she kissed me.

"I've been hearing things in the library today," she said. "There's a whole lot of feeling against you. They're calling you a fake, and I believe a group of them are coming to take it out of you in some way."

"How do you mean?"

"They're planning violence of some kind. You must take care for my sake."

"And for my own," I said with a forced laugh. "But I can't do much until I know what they're planning. If only Satan would come, or at least speak to me, so I'd know what to do."

She caught my hand. "Let me stay with you tonight."

My immediate thought was she mustn't get involved in any trouble, but Kathleen interpreted my worried look differently.

She stepped back. "What have I said? Oh, John, I didn't

mean what you're thinking. I want to wait till we're married, you silly old thing."

"And so do I," I said, as I pulled her to me. "It's funny, isn't it! We've thrown over Christianity, and now we're looking for Christian values in our marriage."

She laughed. "And if you're to be my husband, I'm staying here to be with you in case you're attacked tonight."

"And so you shall," I replied.

CHAPTER 25

The attack didn't come during the night, but a little after dawn when a heavy stone came through my sitting room window and just missed the sofa where I had been sleeping. I called to Kathleen to stay in the bedroom until we knew what was happening.

I put my jacket on, as I was already half dressed, and moved cautiously to the side of the window. I could see a group of about half a dozen men with stocking masks over their faces, and as I looked another stone crashed into the room.

I wasn't anxious to show myself downstairs, and certainly wouldn't open the front door. So I ran upstairs to the bedroom where Kathleen was peering through the gap in the middle of the curtains. The window was half open, and I pulled her aside and pushed the window open further so that I could show myself and speak.

"Who are you, and what do you want?" I shouted.

"We want *you*," one of the men called out.

Another picked up a stone and flung it. It hit the wall.

"You can say anything you want to say from there. I'm listening."

"You're a fraud. You've brought us here, and now we're fed up with this life."

"But you all chose to come," I shouted back.

At this point I heard a noise behind me, and saw Kathleen lying across the bed, completely still. Suddenly I felt energy draining out of me. It was an intensification of what I had felt before when Satan had first materialised. Next moment the blast of a trumpet came from the direction of the village green.

I staggered back to the window. The men had turned away, staring back at the green. In the middle of the green stood a plinth, and on the plinth a tall slim bespectacled figure in a white coat, a typical scientist as imagined by the popular mind. Satan had done the thing properly.

Then I suddenly saw what had happened. Satan had told me he would need to draw on the psychic energies of Kathleen and myself so as to materialise. He had worked on Kathleen's mind to bring us together at the time he wanted, but he had intervened in time to save us from harm by the crowd.

Kathleen was already coming out of her trance, and I caught hold of her hand and raised her up.

"I know," she said. "He's come."

"Are you all right?"

"I think so, more or less. What do we do now?"

"We go out, if you can manage it, and see what's happening. We'll slip out separately, and then you can find me and stay near me."

I looked out of the window again. All the men had vanished. It looked as though every person in the village was hurrying to the green, and we were not slow to join them.

I noticed that no one seemed anxious to step close to the plinth. Obviously, the figure of this super scientist awed them, and I think half of them were afraid that he would turn his magic against them. By now they had almost begun to take for granted the daily magic of goods teleported from earth, quite apart from the mysterious power that had brought us here into ready-built houses. But to come face to face with this worker of miracles was a different matter.

Satan's first words were conciliatory. "You have all wanted to see me, and here I am."

This brought no response from the crowd.

Satan went on, "My deputy John Longstone has told me that you have things to ask me. Is that so?"

"How long have we got to stay here?" a voice called.

This was taken up by, "Yes, yes, tell us," from several in the crowd.

"When you volunteered to come, you were accepted for life."

"We didn't know that at the time."

"You might have guessed. You knew you were taking part in building a good, settled community."

"If we'd been doing it on earth, we could have gone back home when we wanted."

"Yes, and spoilt the whole plan. What's wrong with life on Priam, with everything laid on for your happiness?"

No one answered for a moment, but then Peter Faber

167

spoke. "I'm the doctor, and I'm in touch with the people, and can estimate their reactions. If I may say so, we have too much organised happiness, and many of us have the feeling that what we are *wanting* to do is somehow controlled by Big Brother."

"Doctor," said Satan, "as a well-read man you have heard of Epicurus and the hedonism that is based on his ideas. We are trying to practise a working hedonism, the pursuit of happiness. I am trying to let you have everything that makes for happiness, with restraint on things that might cause unpleasantness."

Someone shouted, "We'd rather go home and take our chances."

"That is impossible," Satan said firmly.

"Then what will be the end of it all?" someone else called.

"You will go on living here and setting up a happy society. Your children will inherit the foundations you have laid."

"And what happens to us when we die?" This was the doctor again.

"Nothing. You will just die with the knowledge that you have contributed something worthwhile to our new society."

"No so-called pie in the sky, then?"

Satan smiled as he turned to the speaker. "You're right, Doctor, no pie in the sky. If you were still on earth you'd find that sensible people have thrown that idea out of the window."

"So you have nothing to promise us after death?"

"Nothing. You, Doctor, know perfectly well that there's no life except in the body and, when the body goes, it's earth to earth, dust to dust."

I was surprised when Peter Faber spoke out. "So the great magician can't promise us eternal life for our souls."

"Exactly. I can't promise an impossibility, and I'm surprised that a doctor would speak of a soul when he's never seen or operated on such a thing in his life."

Someone shouted, "We demand you take us home!" and others joined in.

Satan held up his hand for silence. "You are not going home. *This* is your home, and it's up to you to make it a happy home. I will let you have more if you want, more tokens, and more possessions. You've only to ask my deputy."

Someone called out, "We don't trust John Longstone. We don't like him. We want someone else to be in charge."

Satan replied "I have no complaints about him. But if you are not happy about him — and I want you to be happy — you can deal directly with me. I'm going back. I have other work to do. But I am giving you a statue of myself on this plinth. That will be something for you to see. I will be linked to the statue, and when you come and speak your requests into the trumpet at its feet, I will note everything you say. Trust it as if it were me."

Satan stood there without moving. Those who were closest slowly came nearer. The figure stood motionless. Closer and closer they came, until at last one of them shouted, "He's dead!"

Another stretched out his hand, touched, and quickly

drew his hand back.

"He's not dead," he called out, "he's turned into a statue!"

There was no lack of people pressing forward now to touch. I saw three women kneeling down, and a man joined them. I slipped back home, and Kathleen followed soon afterwards. To my surprise, my window had somehow been mended.

"What do you think about it all?" Kathleen asked.

"I think we have a god on our hands," I said.

For more than half of the village, my words proved to be right. The statue became a centre of veneration. This was helped by the fact that the mouth of the trumpet was so close to the ground that those who came with requests had to go down on their knees to speak into it. From this, it seemed only natural that the worshippers, if I may so call them, ended their petitions by gazing up at the face of the image.

I heard someone say, "We must keep in with him. He might do us harm if we get across him."

After a time I noticed bunches of flowers laid on the plinth.

CHAPTER 26

One day something happened that had some importance for Kathleen and myself. Young Tom Broadwood and Pat Penny, who had been living together, wanted to get properly married, especially as there was a baby on the way. I had been mostly ignored since Satan's visit, which was a blow to my self-esteem, but now these two came to ask me how they could be officially married, since there was no church or register office to apply to.

With my hot line to Satan no longer open, all I could do was advise them to go and speak to the statue. They followed my advice, and the trumpet spoke the answer. They must kneel in front of the statue and declare that they wished to take one another as legally man and wife. They told their friends, and on the appointed day we stood round and watched the solemnisation of the first wedding on Priam.

Kathleen and I discussed it afterwards. We too intended to be married, although for some reason we had gone out of our way to keep our relationship secret.

"I don't know about you," said Kathleen, "but I don't

fancy getting married at Satan's feet."

I agreed. But what was the alternative if we wanted to be properly married? To live together as Tom and Pat had done? We were caught in a trap.

Meanwhile I sensed a change in the atmosphere of life, and there seemed to me to be a steady deterioration. It arose, I believe, from Satan's clear approval of, "Eat, drink, and be merry, for tomorrow you die." Certainly those I've described as "worshippers" at the statue were asking for much more than they needed.

The bank had instructions to increase the allowance of tokens. There was no poverty in the village, and indeed no one had been in need since we had arrived. Now there was a rush for luxuries, with the idea of keeping up with the neighbours. But rivalry didn't bring contentment. There was always the feeling that there must be more to come.

I noticed another group, who took advantage of extras, but who were profoundly dissatisfied with the thought of living and dying on Priam. If they were to die, they wanted first to return to earth, and they were convinced that the superscientist could arrange this by the same method that had brought them here.

I think only the doctor and his wife, beside Kathleen and myself, had any real insight into what was happening. One evening I had to call at the surgery with a septic finger, and after he had finished with me, Peter Faber asked me to sit down while he sat at his desk.

"There aren't any more patients this evening," he began, "so I'd like to have a talk."

"That's fine," I said.

"Well, I'm not happy with the way things are going. Excuse me being blunt, but I have a set of spoilt babies on my hands. They have everything they want, far more than they need, but they're coming to me with all sorts of things wrong. You know what psychosomatic means."

I nodded.

"Some of their ailments are real, some, I believe, are in the mind."

I interrupted. "Why has it happened?"

"Just a theory of mine," he said. "I think they're afraid — basically afraid that they'll die before they've had time to enjoy all they have. They want me to patch them up to keep them going."

"You're probably right," I said. "And maybe some of them are producing an illness to punish themselves for having so much. A hangover from early teachings where God put down the mighty from their seat."

It was his turn to nod agreement. "Tell me, John," he said, "how are you reacting to all this affluence?"

I hesitated before replying. "It may sound ... pious, but I don't think it's making any difference. I've naturally drawn all the tokens I've needed since we've been here, and I don't think I've drawn any extra since our scientist was here."

"I guessed not," said Peter Faber. "It's been the same with my wife and me. But I fancy we're in a minority. I'm afraid I would shock you if I said I sometimes wonder whether the Christian attitude to life may be correct."

"You mean contentment, I take it, not the Christian ideas about God."

"I suppose so, if one can have the one without the other."

There was a ring on the bell, and the doctor rose. "Sounds like another patient after all."

I heard him at the door. It *was* a patient. I said good-bye, and left. I wished he hadn't talked like that.

Soon after this, I was made once more aware of Satan's values. He was evidently quite willing to allow material luxuries, but he was determined to stop some other so-called freedoms which might disrupt his community. From time to time a voice spoke through the trumpet on the statue. The voice named no names, but gave a warning to someone who was doing what was wrong.

If the warning was ignored, an accident happened. Thus a married man who was carrying on with a neighbour's wife, slipped and broke his ankle one night as he was leaving his gate, while simultaneously, as she was getting ready to go out and meet him in the woods, she caught her coat on the kettle and poured a stream of near boiling water on her foot.

A violent husband, who was about to strike his wife, found his arm paralysed, and remain paralysed for a week — when equally suddenly his arm returned to normal. Two teenagers who had been drinking heavily and damaging property, woke up to find themselves blind, again for a week.

At the same time, the voice was naming people for rewards of extra tokens or presents when they had done some act of kindness, such as cooking for an invalid, tidying a garden, or painting a house, without asking for payment — as had happened when Agnes Brown was ill.

CHAPTER 27

The doctor's remarks about Christians worried me more than I had realised at the time. At first I didn't mention them to Kathleen, since I knew she might well take Peter Faber's suggestion seriously. But if we were to be married, we would have to agree on such a vital issue. So I told her one evening.

She responded as I was afraid she would. "Don't you think there may be something in it?"

"Be sensible," I said. "You don't have to be a Christian to believe in self-control. Why, you and I believe in it, don't we? Christians believe that if you're good, self-sacrificing people, you'll have a nice self-indulgent life in heaven."

"Is that entirely fair? When you used to call yourself a Christian, did you have that idea in your mind?"

"To be quite honest, I don't think I did."

"I was never allowed to be a Christian. My father would point to the people coming out of the local church, and tell me they were a lot of hypocrites. He said he could be good without being a Christian. When I was older, I used to wonder what he meant by "good", because I knew he was being unfaithful to my mother. But I've always felt that anyone can be good if they really want to."

I found myself back in my lecturing days. "Christians would say that there is plenty of common ground of morality with non-Christians. Christian morality coincides with what is satisfactory for individuals and community. So others, not just Christians, find by experience that some things are satisfactory, and so they are good, while others are disruptive and bad."

Kathleen nodded. "I see that. That seems to be the principle Satan is working on here. But what puzzles me is how Christianity can claim to be better. I suppose it has something special to do with Jesus, and he sets an example of goodness that satisfies. But is that all?"

"No, there's more than that. Christians believe in … in … a nice cup of tea."

Something was wrong.

"What was I saying? I can't remember. My mind's confused."

Kathleen's eyes were staring, without seeming to see me.

"What's wrong with us?" I shouted. "Our minds are being taken over. We must fight it. Concentrate, Kathleen, concentrate!"

Her voice became slow and quiet. "It's no use, John, we can't." And then, deliberately, and louder, "God, if you exist, stop Satan muddling our minds!"

"No, Kathleen, no!" I cried. "You mustn't say it." But as I spoke, I knew my mind was clear once more.

We sat and looked at each other without speaking for a full minute. She came over to me, and stood with a hand on my shoulder. "Don't be angry with me," she whispered, "it just came out. I couldn't help it."

"I'm not angry, Kathleen. But what is this going to mean? You realise we've challenged Satan. And we can't stop now."

"We can, if I promise never to appeal to God again."

"But after what's happened tonight, you're bound to have some sort of belief in God."

Kathleen stayed silent for some time, obviously deep in thought. "Yes," she said at last, "yes, I'm bound to. God did what we couldn't do ourselves."

"Or could we say that the idea of prayer triggered off a powerful suggestion in both of us?"

"So I'm marrying a professional sceptic and you're marrying a credulous, suggestible woman. Seriously, ought we to go through with it? Aren't we going to find ourselves on different sides?"

"Listen," I said, "we love each other, and we're going to be married."

"But on different sides?"

"No," I said, "but what's happened tonight is too big for us to understand, without thinking out what it means. I love you, Kathleen, but I must be alone now."

"And so must I. I love you too, John, and I'll play fair with you. I promise. So goodnight."

She kissed me, and was gone.

I had a broken night, with Kathleen's words twisting and turning through my brain. "God, if you exist," "God, if you don't exist," "God, if perhaps you exist," "God, I know you don't exist," "God, how do I know you don't exist?" And then, "Satan, I know you exist." And so on and on, in an infinite variety.

Next morning, I discovered something to take my mind off our troubles. During the night the statue of Satan had been pushed off its plinth and was lying broken in several pieces on the ground, with bits that looked as though they had been chipped off by a hammer.

The news quickly got round, and people came out of their houses to see for themselves. Certainly some were frightened. I could tell they were, from the way they shrank back from coming too near. Only a few actually went up to the broken statue and examined it. I went with them.

Someone asked, "Are we going to mend it?"

Another replied, "What's the point? Anyway, it's too big for us to handle, and how could we stick the chipped pieces together?"

The trumpet still lay on the plinth.

"Perhaps that thing will tell us what to do," someone suggested.

"More likely it'll tell us who did it. And I wouldn't want to be in his shoes."

We were still debating, when suddenly the mass began to move. The base glided back on to the plinth, and the other sections climbed into place — like a jigsaw fitted by an invisible giant. Then the chips of stone flew up and placed themselves in the gashes, and behold, the statue was intact once more with every crack perfectly bonded so that no one could tell that the statue had ever been broken. I saw many different reactions.

Some ran for home. Others gazed in awe, and even fell on their knees before the miracle. I walked home thoughtfully, and wondered how Satan would punish those who had vandalised his image.

The surprising thing was that nothing happened. Kathleen and I didn't meet that evening. We both had much to think about. But next evening I went to her house. We both felt rather awkward, and I wondered how we would get round the problem that we had left unsolved two nights before.

To break the ice, I raised a different question. "Why do you think Satan has done nothing about the wrecking of his statue?"

"I've been thinking about that," Kathleen said. "I wonder whether he can make more capital out of its restoration."

"But that wouldn't prevent him from punishing the original vandals. There must have been several involved, to break up a thing like that."

"Do you suppose he doesn't want to call too much attention to what looks like rebellion?"

"Maybe that's it. I wonder how much rebellion there is. Some people didn't mind speaking out when Satan came."

Kathleen hesitated. Then she leaned forward and almost whispered, "Does he think you and I are going to be rebels?"

"I see what you mean. But it's no good whispering, to stop his agents listening to what we're saying. They can hear our voices, however quietly we speak. We just have to talk things through, and take the consequences."

"We'll only have to take the consequences if you come down on my side."

She had a point there. "Kathleen, let's simply say we've got to talk things through."

"Okay, John, so we'll start where our minds got blocked before. And I'll say again, 'God, if you exist, stop Satan muddling our minds.'"

I sensed a change of atmosphere in the room as Kathleen said this. She looked at me. "I was asking you what Christians believe is unique about Jesus. You can at least tell me that, even if you don't believe it. You can surely remember what you used to teach your students."

I seemed to be back again in my study and lecture room, with the many books that I parted with when I realised I no longer believed as a Christian. My mind was clear. "The Christian belief is that Jesus is the promised Messiah, that is the Christ. He is God, who was born of a virgin as man. He died on the cross for our sins, and came alive again in a bodily resurrection. He is now in heaven as God with his Father, and yet lives in his people through his Holy Spirit."

I paused, surprised at the fervency with which I had outlined the faith that I had tried so hard to forget.

Kathleen gazed at me wide-eyed. "Is that what you believed once? Where does it all come from? It sounds too complicated for anyone to make up."

"It's what the Bible says, and you either accept it or reject it. I rejected it."

"Well, if I'm to reject it, I must at least know what I'm rejecting. We can't get a Bible here, that's for sure, but how much can you remember?"

Thus began what would have been called Bible studies if we'd had Bibles. I was surprised to find how much I remembered from the Bible as I talked about the Christian faith. Regularly each evening we began with Kathleen's prayer to a possible God, and then I spoke. The early Christian creeds gave us our subjects.

At first I was careful to raise what I regarded as powerful answers to the Bible statements, but little by little the objections faded into the background and I spoke "as an evangelist", according to Kathleen.

The evening came when Kathleen suddenly surprised me by saying quite quietly, "Do you know, I think I believe it all. Don't you? You've not been bringing out so many objections lately."

I felt startled. Each day I'd had a sense of freedom in explaining the teachings of the Bible, and all sorts of texts and quotations kept coming into my mind, even though I had forgotten them for years. Moreover, we had not felt any interruption from Satan. Kathleen's words jolted me. Did I, after all, really believe what I had been saying? My answer seemed to be forced out of me.

"Yes, I think I do."

"Then are we both Christians?"

"We both believe the Christian creeds, but I don't think that belief *about* Jesus Christ is enough. After all, Satan must believe God exists, and it's not doing him any good."

"Then God is real," Kathleen said. A simple statement.

I nodded slowly, as the full force of her statement came through to me. "We must believe *in* Jesus, trust him, have faith in him, and ask him to forgive us."

Kathleen looked me full in the face. "Then let's trust him together."

I shook my head. "You can trust him, Kathleen. I can't. I've gone too far with Satan. I daren't ask Jesus to forgive me."

"Try, John, try! You *want* to be forgiven. You *want* to become a Christian again. Surely he'll accept you."

She fell on her knees. "Jesus," she said, "John and I want to trust you. You died for us. Help us to trust you, and make us true Christians."

I couldn't let Kathleen speak for me. I joined in with her prayer and made it my own.

In that moment light flashed into my whole being, and all I could hear was Kathleen's voice calling, "Thank you, thank you, Lord Jesus!"

I repeated the words that she kept calling out.

How long we knelt side by side, calling and calling, I can't say. But what I remember afterwards was being in each other's arms, and telling whoever was listening, "We're Christians, we're Christians!"

It was very late before we parted, and I think Kathleen had as broken a night as I had.

"John, you look different," she said, as I drew her into the house later that day. Her face shone with a new look.

"And you look different too," I said, as I kissed her.

That evening Kathleen raised a point that had also been

in my mind. "Now I'm a Christian, John, you must baptise me. You've already been baptised, but I haven't been."

"I've been thinking along the same lines," I replied. "In any case, we'll have to let the others know we're Christians. And I suppose your baptism will be a good start."

She nodded. "Will you baptise me, then?"

"Yes," I said, "but Satan will probably try to stop us."

"But we'll go through with it, and if we pray against him as Christians I'm sure it will be all right."

"We both seem to be thinking of a public baptism. I could baptise you here privately, of course."

"I suppose so. But I want to confess my faith in Jesus publicly."

We talked a bit more before deciding that I would announce that there would be a baptism in the river where it ran into the lake, and it would be at six o'clock tomorrow evening. I drew up several notices, and after dark posted them up in the village. Up until now we had done our best to keep our attachment secret. Whether we had been at all successful I cannot say, but now both our names were on the notices. I don't know how far our prayers had kept Satan from discovering what we'd been doing.

My belief is that God had been answering by drawing, as it were, a veil over us, and our conversion took Satan by surprise. But a public notice could not be hidden, and it was not surprising that Kathleen and I were both threatened during the day.

When I passed the statue, the voice of the trumpet thundered, "*No Christians on Priam!*" The sound rang through the village.

Kathleen came to me at about half past five. She looked nervous.

"Are you sure you want to go through with it?" I asked.

"Yes, if you are. We'll be marked out from now onwards. You realise that, don't you."

"We'll fight it together," I said. "It's time to go now."

"First we'll pray," Kathleen said quietly, and together we repeated the Lord's Prayer, with its petition, "Deliver us from evil," before stepping out into the street.

As we came near to the pool, we saw a crowd of people waiting for us. Some by the pool were obviously there out of curiosity. But another group moved across the track to bar our way. Kathleen took my arm and we continued to move forward. The group parted, and we walked between them.

They began to shout, "No Christians here!" and one voice called out, "Throw them in the lake!" Someone spat at us, and I dodged a blow to my face.

It might have gone badly with us, but at that moment a man leaped out from the back of the crowd and began to rave obscenities. His face was so horribly contorted that I didn't recognise who he was. Foam ran down his beard as he waved his arms frantically in the air. Everyone turned to stare at him, then pushed back to avoid him.

Someone shouted, "He's mad!"

The man stopped, and stared at the crowd. "I'm not mad! *These* are the mad ones!" He stood right up against me and pointed his finger. His face dribbled against mine.

Kathleen shrank behind me. I was trembling. Then I remembered, and I called out, "In the Name of Jesus Christ I command you, evil spirit, to come out of him!"

185

The man dropped at my feet, and lay motionless on the ground.

"He's dead," someone called, and they all clustered round while Kathleen and I moved to the side and went quickly down to the pool.

There was no further obstruction, and we went together into the water.

I asked one question. "Kathleen, are you a Christian?"

She replied unhesitatingly. "I believe in Jesus Christ, the Son of God, who died for me and was raised again for me."

So I baptised her in the Name of Father, Son and Holy Spirit.

When we came out of the pool the doctor was bending over the man who had been possessed, and those who had threatened us were watching the man as he tried to sit up. The groups on the bank, who had seen the baptism let us through, and the others ignored us as we passed them. We said nothing, but made our way to my house.

We had half expected further trouble, but nothing happened.

CHAPTER 28

From this time, the community began to break up. The statue was thrown down on two successive nights, and each time it was miraculously repaired and replaced. There was constant quarrelling over possessions, and demands for more tokens. Rival groups and gangs formed, and even children were drawn in, and went for one another. Several times there were fights in the street. But, above all, there were constant grumbles over not being able to return to earth.

Kathleen and I were not attacked, but nobody would have much to do with us. I announced a meeting to discuss the claims of Jesus Christ, but nobody came. I even felt moved to speak of Christ on the green, but I was speaking into empty air. I was unable to see what the end would be.

When the end came, it came suddenly.

One morning the sound of the trumpet rang through the village. The voice was harsh and scolding. "You have all been on test, and you have failed me, so you will be sent back to earth. You have had all you needed for a good life

187

here on Priam, and you have let me down. There are even professed Christians among you. Yes, *Christians!*"

Satan paused, probably hoping that the crowd would be so angry that they would attack us. But the people seemed more interested in the prospect of returning home than in bothering with us.

"You have said you wanted to go home to earth, and so you shall. I command you to come out on the green, and at midday you will return. But you can take nothing with you except the clothes you are wearing. Any who fail to come to the green will be left alone with no further help. The planet will once more be empty. There will be no more supplies."

The voice rang through the village. People ran out of their houses, and the voice repeated what it had said before. This time there was an addition.

"You may be wondering how things have changed on earth since you have been here, but you have no need to worry. When you return, you will be back at the precise moment when you left the earth. You have been outside earthly time. I shall block your memories so that all that has happened on Priam will be as though it has never been. You will think that you were enticed into an experiment that failed, as you find yourselves still sitting in your homes. But you will not remember how you came to be involved. There will be no letters left about the experiments."

Satan repeated the speech several times.

Within a few minutes, Kathleen was round at my house. She seemed terribly agitated. "What are we going to do, John?" she asked, grabbing my hand.

"I suppose we'll go back like the rest."

"Then, if we forget everything, we'll lose each other."

"Surely we'll be able to find each other again."

"But, John, if we forget, I won't know anything about you, and won't even look for you, and you won't look for me."

She was crying on my shoulder.

"Suppose we don't go back," I said. "If we don't go out on the green, we'll be left here. That's what Satan said. Could you stay here with me?"

She looked up. "Yes, yes, why shouldn't we stay here? We won't put ourselves under Satan to take us back to earth."

"Then come in. It's not ten o'clock yet. We'll stay here, and I think we should pray together."

"When we're alone, do you think God will let us marry?"

"Adam and Eve lived together as man and wife in Eden. So God must have married them."

So we prayed. We made tea. We talked. We watched from the window to see people collecting on the green. Some danced with excitement. Others walked around slowly, I imagine hesitant about returning.

Time moved slowly at first, and then quickly, as midday drew near. At five minutes to twelve they were all there, except for Dr Faber and his wife who came running out on to the green with barely two minutes to spare. The doctor held a book in his hands.

I watched alternately the clock on the mantelpiece and the crowd outside. Kathleen clung to me, until with half a minute to go she said, "I'm frightened, John. Perhaps we should go after all."

"Listen," I said, "it's too late now. We can't be on the green in time. Besides, we don't want to go and then forget each other. Look!"

The clock struck, and where the green had been crowded there was now just grass. We didn't see them go. They vanished. We two were alone.

"Come," I said, "let's go and see."

I noticed something lying on the grass. We went over to it. It was the book that the doctor had been holding. I picked it up. It was a diary he'd kept spasmodically since he'd been on Priam. We wandered into several of the houses. Everything was in place.

"I wonder what's happened to the ones who died," Kathleen said. "Did they come alive again and go back with all the others? Is my father with them?"

"I don't know. We'll have a look at the graves of the people we buried."

We walked out of the village to see, although of course there had been no grave for Kathleen's father. He had simply disappeared, along with Joan Stuckey. Where we had buried the dead the graves were open, just holes in the ground.

I murmured, "So they too have gone back to where they were when we all left the earth."

As we came back to the village, we saw a man coming towards us down the street.

"Heavens!" said Kathleen, clutching my arm tighter, "Someone else didn't go."

"So we're not left on our own," I said bitterly, resenting

sharing the planet and our life together. "Do you recognise him?"

He was nearer now.

"No, I don't. Oh, John, could it be someone from Satan?"

The person spoke. His voice was gentle. "Peace to you. My Master has sent me to take you back to the earth."

"He's from God," I whispered.

"You two Christians did well not to let Satan take you home, but you cannot stay here. The difference will be that you will remember everything when you return."

He looked at the book that I was still clutching.

"Keep that book. It will help you when you write the story of what has happened here on Priam."

"So," I said, "you're an angel sent from God."

"That is so, but I have been with you ever since you first prayed. Did you wonder why Satan didn't interfere when you spoke together of God's truth? I put a ring around you to block his knowledge of what you were doing, and I stood by you both at the baptism."

"Thank you," said Kathleen. "I wondered why we were so free."

"You took a step of faith in God, and that gave you freedom. But now we must not delay. Kathleen, your father is back home and looking for you. John, I shall take you to your home, instead of to the ancient stone circle from which you departed. You will see Kathleen again tomorrow."

Kathleen and I turned and looked at each other.

I said to the angel, "We can be properly married then?"

He smiled. "Of course."

As I looked, his face and body shivered and blurred. A moment of intense darkness, and I was alone in my room back on earth. The doctor's book was still in my hand, but Kathleen had gone.

The clock on the mantelpiece said twelve o'clock. I switched on the radio. The lunchtime news reader said it was June 24th and the news was the same as when I had left. Time had definitely stood still.

Kathleen arrived early next morning, and we fell into each other's arms. She had been worried that she would never find me, as stupidly we had not exchanged addresses. But a search through the electoral roll in the library where she worked before joining us on Priam, had given my name and address.

"It's true! We're free!" we almost shouted, waltzing round the room.

"You know," said Kathleen, "I feel that we've come out of darkness into light."

I agreed. "I don't think we realised how terrible it was to be under Satan's power."

We talked for an hour, and then Kathleen suggested we should go to see her father. I recognised him at once, but to him I was a total stranger.

"You two have kept very quiet," he said. "Kathleen only told me this morning that a Mr John Longstone was coming round to ask for her hand in marriage. Well, I must agree, but goodness knows who'll look after me now. I'll have to get married again, I suppose." He winked at me.

I need not go on with the story. We had a quiet wedding, with Mr Ryecroft giving Kathleen away. He and Kathleen's late mother had no brothers or sisters, so there were no relatives to come, but only a few friends.

Sadly, only a month or two later, Mr Ryecroft was taken seriously ill and died within a few days. But before then Kathleen and I had been able to speak to him of Jesus Christ, and I am convinced that he died as a Christian. He said he had been influenced by the love he could now see in Kathleen's life.

It has taken me some time to complete this book, and of course I've changed all the names in case any of our fellow travellers should read it. Well, not all the names, because there was no point in changing Mr Ryecroft's.

I asked Kathleen whether I should omit all reference to his involvement in the murder of Bill Stuckey on Priam, but she said No, her father had become a Christian shortly after his return and would have been forgiven not only for the murder — of which of course he had no memory — but also for repenting of his womanizing past.

I look back with horror when I think of that house with the locked door and shuttered windows — how I went in with Satan's key and tried to discover his secrets. All I want now is to know Jesus Christ better and better each day, and to love him more and more.

With regard to ourselves, we now have a boy, and Kathleen tells me we can expect another baby in the spring. One reason why this book has taken so long is that the bishop has allowed me to resume my orders, and as a part-time clergyman I've been doing some lecturing and tutoring in a nearby theological college.

I lecture in Christian doctrine, but the principal has taken a strong exception to some of the things I've said about Satan and the world of spirits. He doesn't believe in a personal devil.

I must give him a copy of this book.

CHRISTIANS AND THE SUPERNATURAL
By J STAFFORD WRIGHT

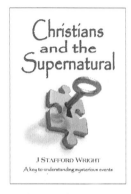

There is an increasing interest and fascination in the paranormal today. To counteract this, it is important for Christians to have a good understanding of how God sometimes acts in mysterious ways, and be able to recognize how he can use our untapped gifts and abilities in his service. We also need to understand how the enemy can tempt us to misuse these gifts and abilities, just as Jesus was tempted in the wilderness.

In this single volume of his two previously published books on the occult and the supernatural (*Understanding the Supernatural* and *Our Mysterious God*) J Stafford Wright examines some of the mysterious events we find in the Bible and in our own lives. Far from dismissing the recorded biblical miracles as folk tales, he is convinced that they happened in the way described, and explains why we can accept them as credible.

The writer says: *When God the Holy Spirit dwells within the human spirit, he uses the mental and physical abilities which make up a total human being . . . The whole purpose of this book is to show that the Bible does make sense.*

And this warning: *The Bible, claiming to speak as the revelation of God, and knowing man's weakness for substitute religious experiences, bans those avenues into the occult that at the very least are blind alleys that obscure the way to God, and at worst are roads to destruction.*

ISBN 13: 9-780-9525-9564-9
222 pages 5.25 x 8 inches £8.95 and US $12.95
Available from bookstores and major internet sellers

ALSO FROM WHITE TREE
PUBLISHING
BIBLE PEOPLE
REAL PEOPLE
By J STAFFORD WRIGHT
In a fascinating look at real people, J Stafford Wright shows his love and scholarly knowledge of the Bible as he brings the characters from its pages to life in a memorable way.

✓ Read this book through from A to Z, like any other title.
✓ Dip in and discover who was who in personal Bible study.
✓ Check the names when preparing a talk or sermon.

The good, the bad, the beautiful and the ugly — no one is spared. This is a book for everyone who wants to get to grips with the reality that is in the pages of the Bible, the Word of God.

With the names arranged in alphabetical order, the Old and New Testament characters are clearly identified so that the reader is able to explore either the Old or New Testament people on the first reading, and the other Testament on the second.

Those wanting to become more familiar with the Bible will find this is a great introduction to the people inhabiting the best selling book in the world, and those already familiar with the Bible will find everyone suddenly becomes much more real — because these people *are* real. This is a book to keep handy and refer to frequently while reading the Bible.

ISBN 13: 9-780-9525-9565-6
310 pages 6 x 9 inches £9.95 and US $14.95
Available from bookstores and major internet sellers
Previously published as *Dictionary of Bible People*

MAKES A GREAT GIFT!

Made in the USA
Charleston, SC
17 October 2012